The MYSTERIOUS BENEDICT SOCIETY
Mr. Benedict's Book of Perplexing Puzzles, Elusive Enigmas, and Curious Conundrums

# The Mysterious Benedict Society

## Mr. Benedict's Book of Perplexing Puzzles, Elusive Enigmas, and Curious Conundrums

TRENTON LEE STEWART

Illustrations by
Diana Sudyka



Megan Tingley Books
LITTLE, BROWN AND COMPANY
New York Boston

I wish to thank the writer and riddler Josh Greenhut,
the excellent editors Julie Scheina and Megan Tingley,
the conscientious copy editor Barbara Bakowski, and
the clever ancient persons who invented paper and ink.
This book would not exist without them.



Little, Brown and Company

Hachette Book Group
237 Park Avenue, New York, NY 10017
Visit our website at www.lb-kids.com

Little, Brown and Company is a division of Hachette Book Group, Inc.
The Little, Brown name and logo are trademarks of Hachette Book Group, Inc.



First Edition: October 2011



Library of Congress Cataloging-in-Publication Data

Stewart, Trenton Lee.
The mysterious Benedict society : Mr. Benedict's book of perplexing puzzles, elusive enigmas, and curious conundrums / by Trenton Lee Stewart ; illustrated by Diana Sudyka.
p. cm. — (The Mysterious Benedict Society)
ISBN 978-0-316-18193-8
1. Puzzles—Juvenile literature. 2. Riddles, Juvenile. 3. Amusements—Juvenile literature.
I. Title.
GV1493.S813 2011
793.73—dc22 2011010259

10 9 8 7 6 5 4 3 2 1

SC

Printed in China

Book Design by Georgia Rucker Design

# Dear Reader,

I am aware that certain individuals have become acquainted with the adventures — and even the personal stories — of the remarkable children who call themselves the Mysterious Benedict Society. Furthermore, it is my understanding that these individuals have developed a wish to see their own wits tested, much as the wits of the Society members were tested before the Society was formed. If you are reading these words, it is likely you are just such an individual. Therefore, I urge you to put on your thinking cap (or if you are already wearing your thinking cap, to adjust it so that it rests most comfortably upon your head), for with the aid — indeed, the considerable contributions — of the Society members themselves, as well as a few of my associates, I have compiled the manual you now hold in your hands: a compressed and highly portable collection of mental challenges. May you find them rewarding!

Best regards,

**Mr. Benedict**

P.S. If, perchance, this volume is not part of your personal collection, please complete the exercises in a separate notebook so that others who wish to attempt these challenges may do so.

She continued handing out the test. Child after child received it with trembling fingers, and child after child, upon looking at the questions, turned pale, or red, or a subtle shade of green. By the time the pencil woman dropped the pages upon his desk, dread was making Reynie's stomach flop like a fish.

And for good reason —

the questions were impossible.

# Table of Contents

## PUZZLES, ENIGMAS, AND CONUNDRUMS

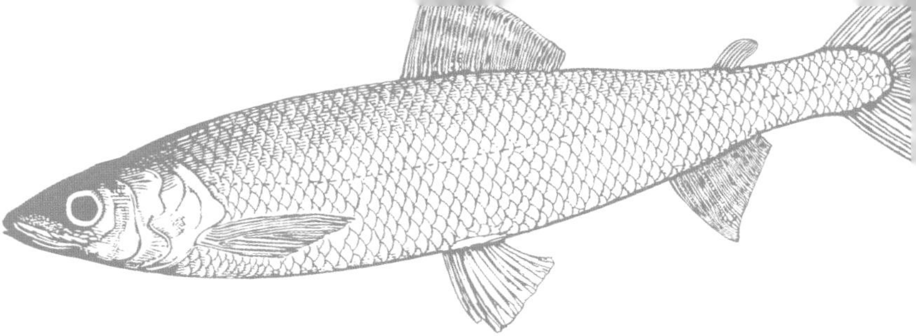

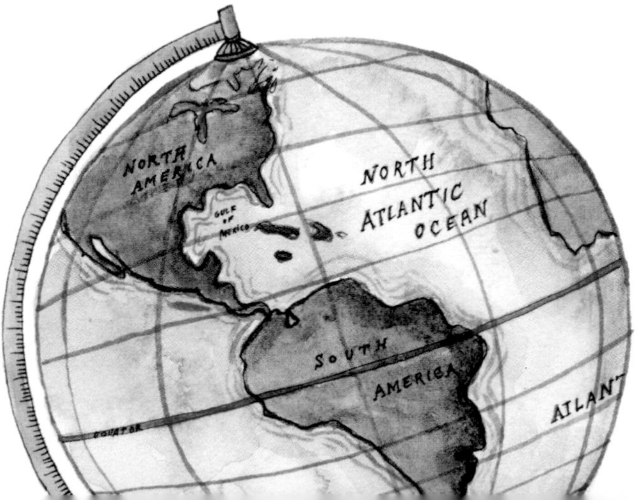
NORTH AMERICA
NORTH ATLANTIC OCEAN
SOUTH AMERICA
ATLANT

## ARCHIVAL MATERIALS

## Helpful Resources



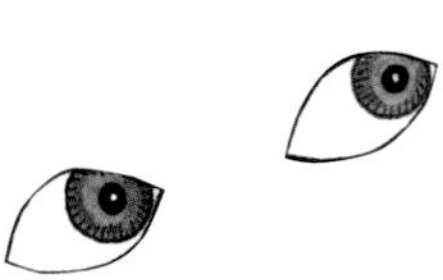

"The Mysterious Benedict Society,"

Constance said, rising as she spoke.

Then she left the room,
apparently convinced that
no more discussion was necessary.

And, as it turned out, she was right.

*What brought together the members of the Mysterious Benedict Society? One might say it was our advertisement. I would argue, however, that there was also something else, something unspoken hiding in plain sight, which most had failed to detect. Can you see what it was?*

# CLASSIFIED ADVERTISEMENTS

HELP  ANTED
Administrative
Assistant
Only those who dare not defy need apply.

**THE INSTITUTE OF ACCOUNTING**

---

EMERGENCY
HYGIENE
SEMINAR

Are you touching this newspaper right now? Because it's covered in germs!
Sickness lurks like a hungry predator in every nook and cranny. Learn  ow to protect yourself.

Mondays at 8 PM

THE
ASCOT TOWER

---

SICK
OF BAD
APPLES?

We are not and never have been government-run!
Bring the kiddies and get our worm-free guarantee.

**JIMMY'S**

APPLE P CKING &
CORN MAZE
THE ORCHARD IN
THE COUNTRY

---

Call 555-1299
to place
**Your Advertisement**

HERE

---

FREE
MARKET-
ING ADVICE

I can't control myself!
Is your business being hit hard by the Emergency?
Well, today's your lucky day! Listen up and get my FREE MARKET-ing advice. Not just in any case, but only in certain cases!
That's right, cal now to get you FREE MARKET ing advice. Only avail able in certain case .

Call
555-7655
**Now!**

CALL 555-1299

YOUR

LAWN CONTROL

You grow it, we mow it!

Weed Removal
Tree Pruning
Large Selection of  esticides

LOOK FOR US IN *YOUR* NEIGHBORHOOD

TAKE MORE TIME TO RELAX

Work Longer Hours
Find Out How!

Don't wast  another moment,
Call
RANDALL & RAYMOND, INC.

YOUR ADVE TISEMENT HERE

Make sure people get the message!

*Stonetown Times, Advertising Department*

REYNALDO'S

TV & RADIO REPAIR

Never miss a transmission again.

All makes and mod ls.
24/7 Emergency Service

ARE YOU A GIFTED CHILD LOOKING FOR SPECIAL OPPORTUNITIES?

.................................

Tests administered at 777 Maiden Avenue, Stonetown Harbor. Attend one of these sessions if you are interested.

Saturday at 8:00 AM, 9:30 AM, or 11:00 AM

Sunday at 8: 00 AM, 9:30 AM, or 11:00 AM

NOT MISSING

Dog recently departed. Black-and-white French bulldog, answers to the name Romeo. We a e sure he is fine.

Call 555-1299 to place **Your Advertisement**

HERE

# The Message in the Advertisements

*Sometimes it is better to say nothing.*

*I have no character*
*(Though I drop them in print)*
*I'm inside your head*
*(Let me give you a hint)*
*I'm quiet and soft*
*(Not blaring and loud)*
*I prompt, then I sweep*
*To control the crowd*

What am I?

_ _ _ _ _ _ _ _ _

# DOTS and DASHES

*Morse code is one of the most reliable methods of*
*secret communication.*
*It may also be one of the most commonly misunderstood.*

.-..  .  ..-.  -  .--  .-.  ---  -.  --.

Only one of the Morse codes found in the
Helpful Resources at the back of this book is
the International Morse Code, as agreed upon in 1865
at the International Telegraphy Congress in Paris, France.

Which code is the right one? Enter the page number
of the official Morse code below.

___ ___ ___

# The Maze of Pages

*Dozens of variations on the maze*
*were created over the years.*
*This was one of the first.*

Navigate your way through the following pages in the correct order. Should you find yourself stuck in the middle, you are headed in the right direction.

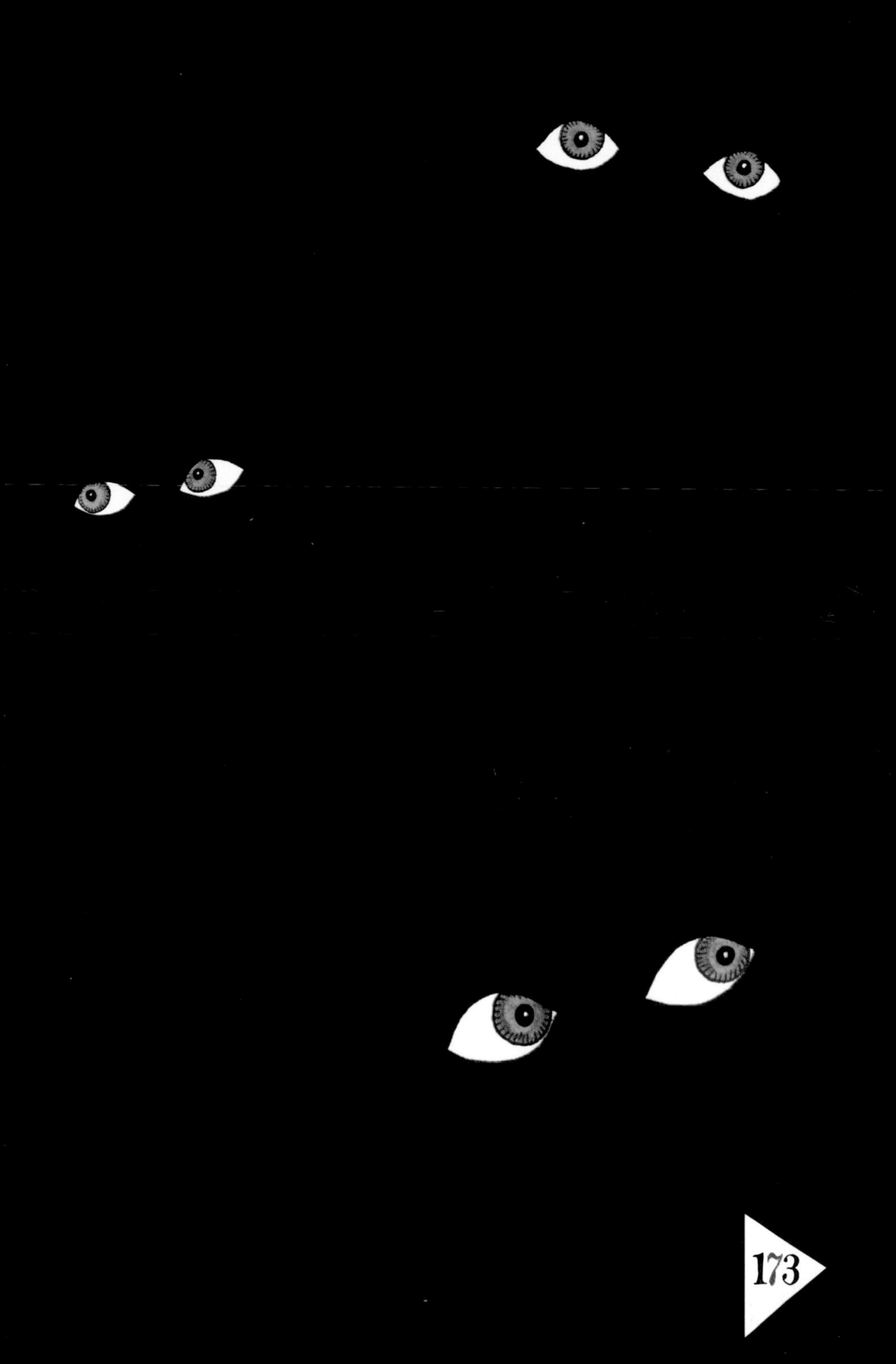

151

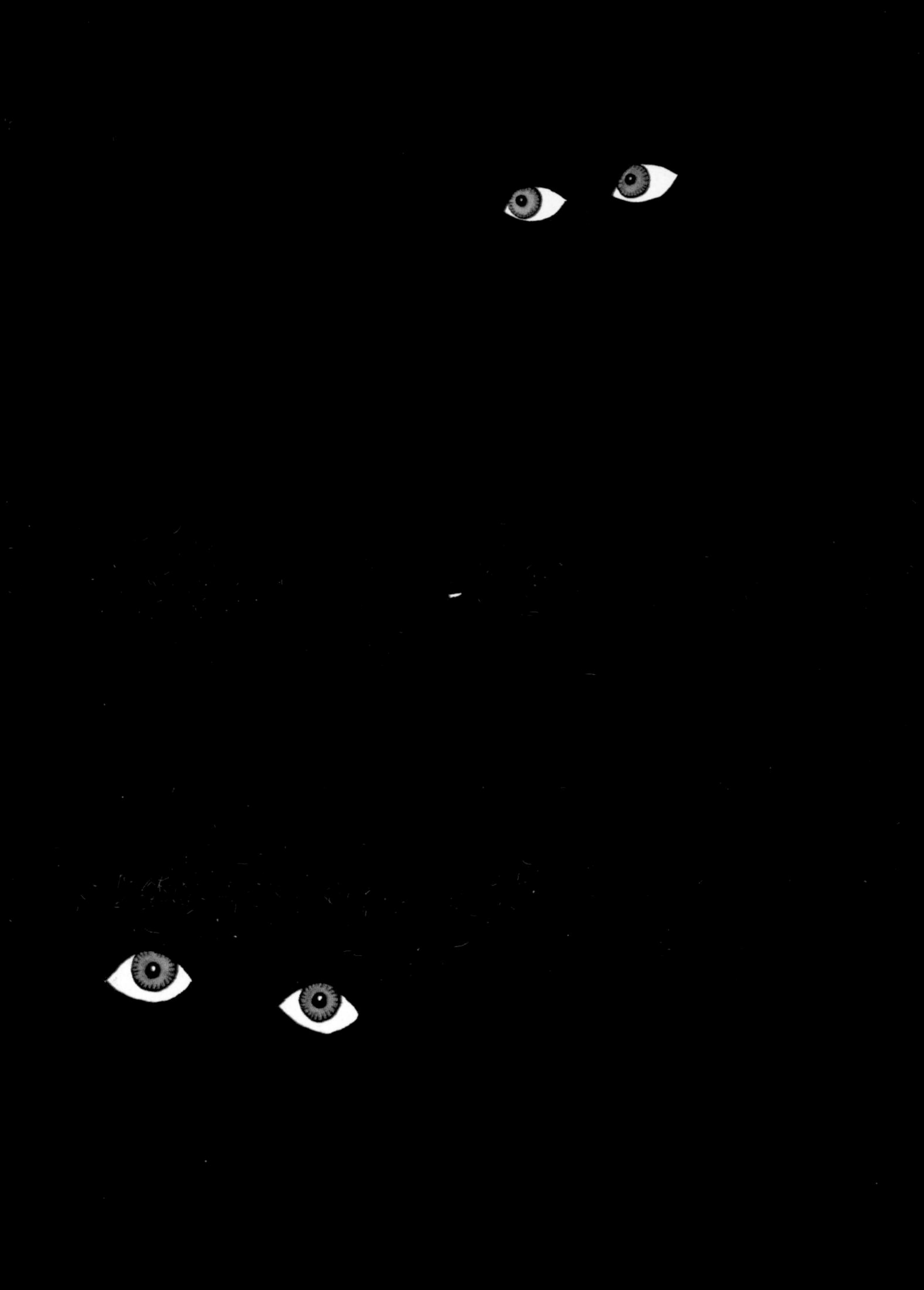

125

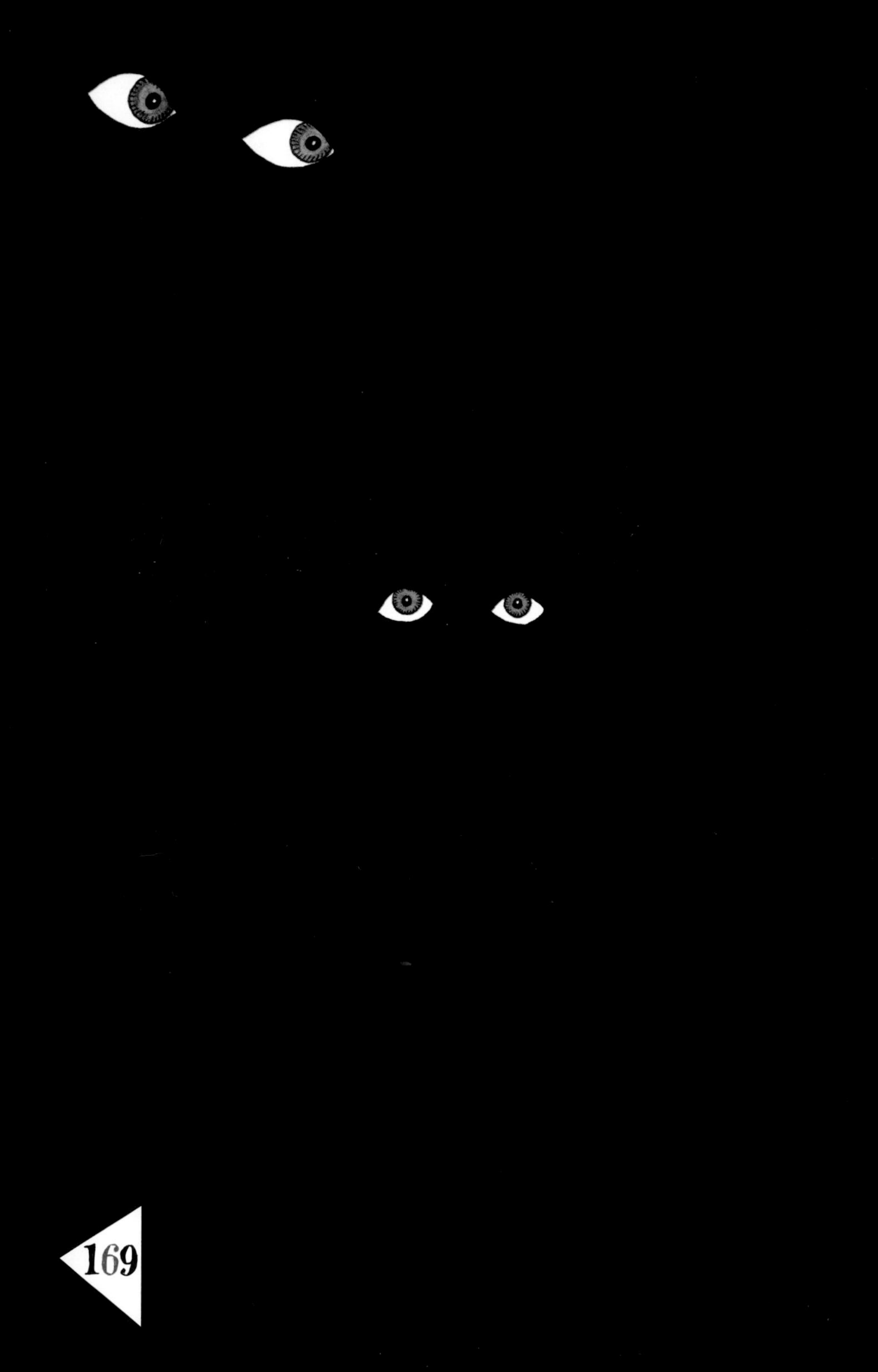

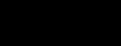

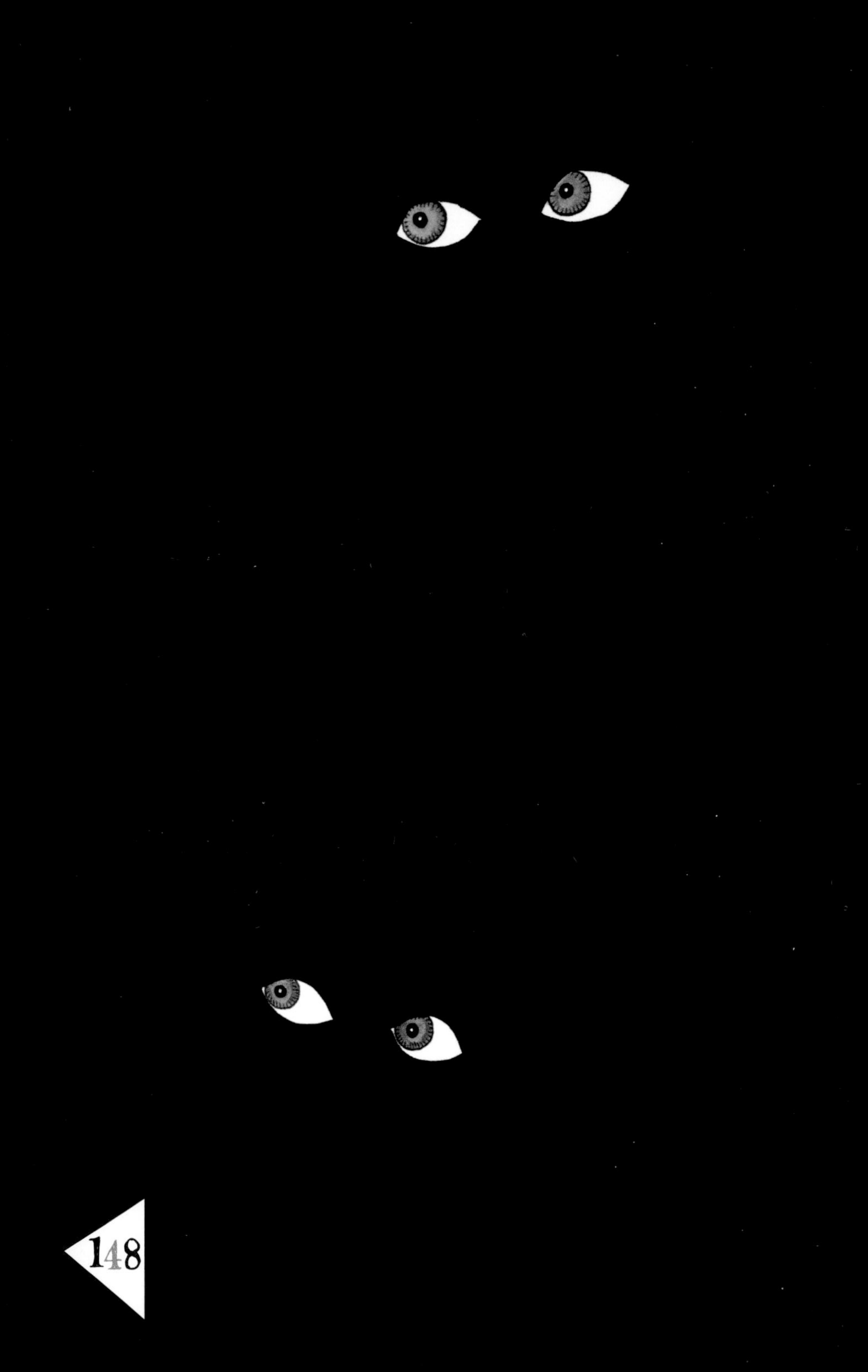

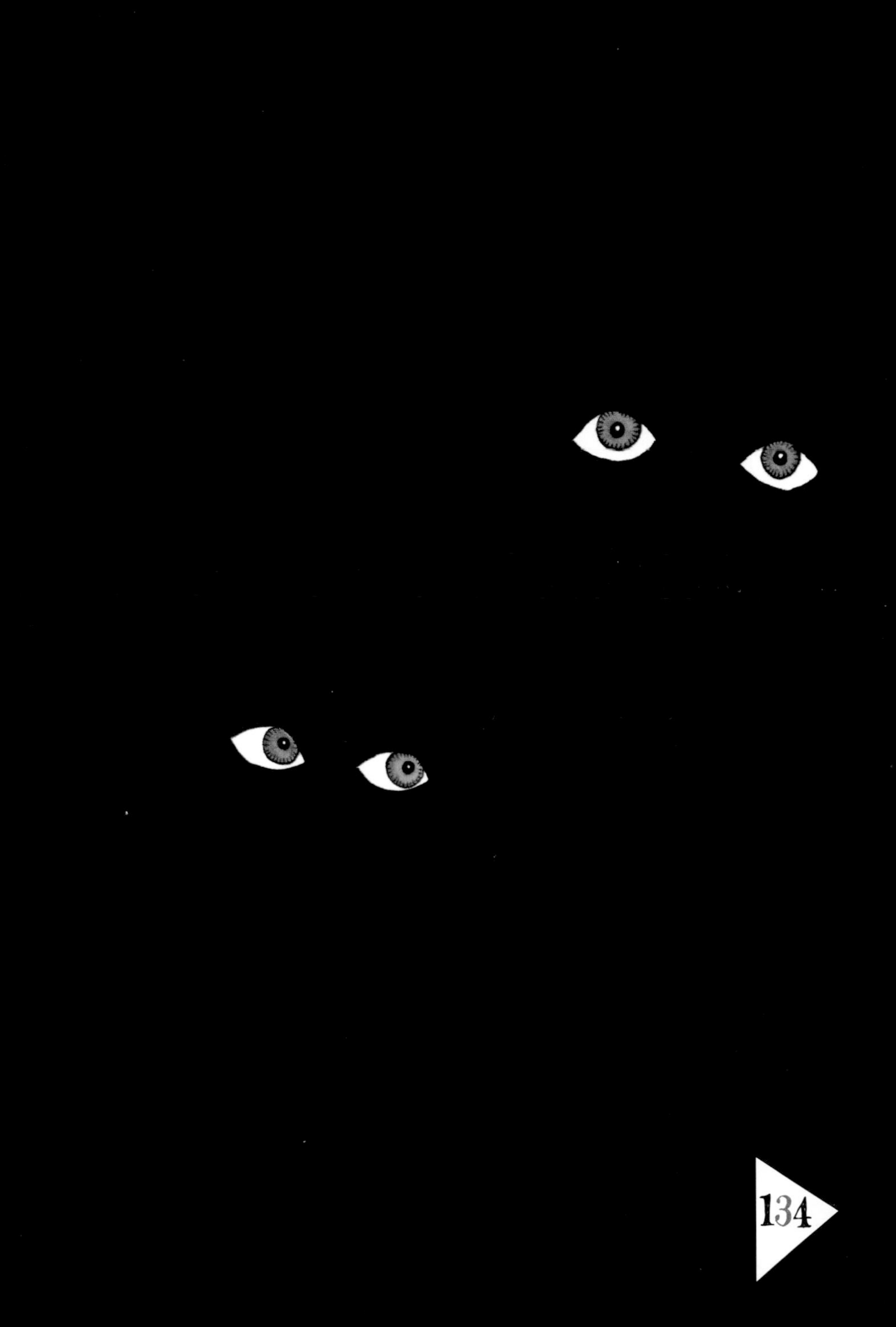
134

*When Reynie was ten years old, Miss Perumal persuaded the director of Stonetown Orphanage to allow him to enter a local chess tournament. Her pride when Reynie won his age-group that day may have been matched only by my own for another, older competitor in that tournament.*

# Reynie Muldoon Perumal

**FOUNDING MEMBER,**
**THE MYSTERIOUS BENEDICT SOCIETY**

*Achievements* Learned Tamil; attained highest possible score on Mr. Benedict's tests; correctly guessed Mr. Curtain's secret password; consistently led friends with grace and wisdom against all odds

*Expertise* Problem solving

*Habits* Pacing when thinking

*History* Orphaned as an infant; formerly resided at Stonetown Orphanage

*Family* Miss Perumal, former tutor at Stonetown Orphanage, and her mother

If you have arrived here
after a long journey,
congratulations are
in order.

Record the route you followed.

___ ___ ___

___ ___ ___

___ ___ ___

___ ___ ___

___ ___ ___

___ ___ ___

___ ___ ___

"Eavesdropping!" Number Two hissed, crossing her arms.

"Without *me*!" Constance said, doing the same.

Milligan came along the hallway behind them. Playfully tapping Kate on the head with a bundle of papers, he said, "This is hardly appropriate behavior, young lady. Spies have *rules*, you know."

*These excerpts from* The Exhaustive Encyclopedia of Sleep, *Fourth Edition, Volume 2, by Dr. Marlene Sternwahl and Marlowe Kandelshaw, provide some useful insights concerning my condition, as well as other difficult questions.*

## OLD-HAG SYNDROME

Of all symptoms commonly afflicting those with narcolepsy, a chronic condition whose sufferers fall asleep at inappropriate times, sometimes triggered by intense emotion and consequential cataplexy, perhaps the most terrifying is sleep paralysis, also known as Old-Hag Syndrome, a name thought to have originated in the folk tradition of Newfoundland and Labrador, the Canadian province divided by the Strait of Belle Isle, because it causes its victims to feel as if some dark presence is holding them down and preventing them from moving in any way. Difficulty breathing and heightened anxiety are characteristic. In duration such episodes may range from several seconds to many minutes, and may be accompanied by vivid hallucinations of a specter or hag sitting directly on the sufferer's chest. Reports of this terrifying phenomenon are found in most cultures, such as in Malta, one of the world's smallest and most densely populated countries, where according to superstition one must place a piece of silverware under one's pillow to prevent haunting by an evil spirit while asleep.

## DUSKWORT

Duskwort, or *Translucidus somniferum*, is a plant allegedly capable of instantly putting all who come in contact with it to sleep, although there is little evidence of its existence, beyond appearances in a handful of ancient Germanic texts and Nordic folktales, which suggest that it may once have grown in certain alpine tundra regions, such as those in northern Europe, and on the Scandinavian peninsula, which comprises Norway and Sweden. In perhaps the most famous duskwort legend, a band of invading Vikings discovers an entire village of people who have suddenly fallen asleep after merely inhaling smoke from a fire into which a tiny bit of the plant has been thrown. An especially large patch of duskwort was rumored to exist somewhere in the Russian taiga, the largest area of boreal forest in the world. So powerful was the plant thought to have been that references to its appearance, or to where it might be found, were excised from ancient texts.

## SLEEPTHINKING

Rapid eye movement (REM) sleep, that period of sleep during which electrical activity in the brain is highest, is thought to aid in the solving of difficult problems, because the brain's neurons are more likely to make nonlinear, associative connections, as determined by researchers at the Sleep Institute of Belize, the northernmost Central American nation. Interestingly, those who suffer from narcolepsy access REM sleep in a matter of minutes, far more quickly than other subjects, who routinely take more than ninety minutes to reach this stage.

# Too Close TO CALL

*As Constance will attest, images often prove more effective than words when attempting to put an idea in someone's head.*

Each of these transmissions is intended for a different recipient. Can you determine whom?

**1.** _ _ _ _ _ _ _ _ _

**2.** ___ ___ ___ ___ ___ ___ ___ ___ ___ ___

**3.** ◯ ___ ___ ___ ___ ___ ___ ___ ___ ___ ___ ___ ___ ___

**4.** ___ ___ ___ ___ ___ ___ ___ ___

# GEOGRAPHY TEST

*You should be able to answer these questions in your sleep.*

**1.** Which of the following is one of the world's smallest and most densely populated countries?

a) MALTA

b) BRAZIL

c) LUXEMBOURG

d) PANAMA

e) LICHTENSTEIN

**2.** Where is the Strait of Belle Isle?

a) ALASKA

b) GIBRALTAR

c) NEWFOUNDLAND AND LABRADOR

d) THE PHILIPPINES

e) SCOTLAND

**3.** What countries compose the Scandinavian peninsula?

a) Norway, Finland, and Belgium

b) Belgium and the Netherlands

c) Norway and Sweden

d) Finland and Norway

e) Norway, Sweden, Finland, and Iceland

**4.** What is the largest area of boreal forest on earth?

a) Amazon rain forest

b) Amana Reserve

c) Redwood forest

d) Sundarbans mangrove forest

e) Russian taiga

**5.** What is the northernmost country in Central America?

a) Honduras

b) Belize

c) Argentina

d) Mexico

e) Congo

*This article appeared in the* Stonetown Times *a matter of weeks before Sticky came into our lives. It illustrates something that most of us have never known of him before. (If that makes you scratch your head, you have found it.)*

STONETOWN TIMES

# SEARCH CONTINUES FOR QUIZ CHAMP

Eleven-year-old undefeated quiz champion George Washington, also known as "Sticky" due to his remarkable ability to retain information, remains departed today after running away from home more than two weeks ago. In a note left behind for his parents, the quiz whiz said, "The psychological pressure has become inordinate." In other words, experts say, he was stressed out from winning too much. Over the last four years, Washington won nearly fifty quiz competitions, amassing thousands of dollars in cash and prizes for his family.

George "Sticky" Washington, middle, ran away from home more than two weeks ago.

# George "Sticky" Washington

**FOUNDING MEMBER,**
**THE MYSTERIOUS BENEDICT SOCIETY**

*Achievements* Memorized the Stonetown Library catalog; braved the Whisperer for the sake of his friends; helped save Mr. Benedict's life

*Expertise* Ability to read exceptionally quickly and recall every word *exactly* (as a result, can read and write, though not necessarily speak, most major languages)

*Habits* Polishing spectacles when nervous; can become confused under pressure

*History* Former quiz-show champion; ran away from home after overhearing conversation between his mother and father

*Family* Mr. and Mrs. Washington, his concerned and loving parents

# The Ten Man Briefcase

*Rather than turn away from terrible things, it is our responsibility to learn from them. Milligan suggested this exercise after examining a briefcase he personally removed from a Ten Man.*

Your task is deceptively simple. Pack the following items in the briefcase so that all of them fit.

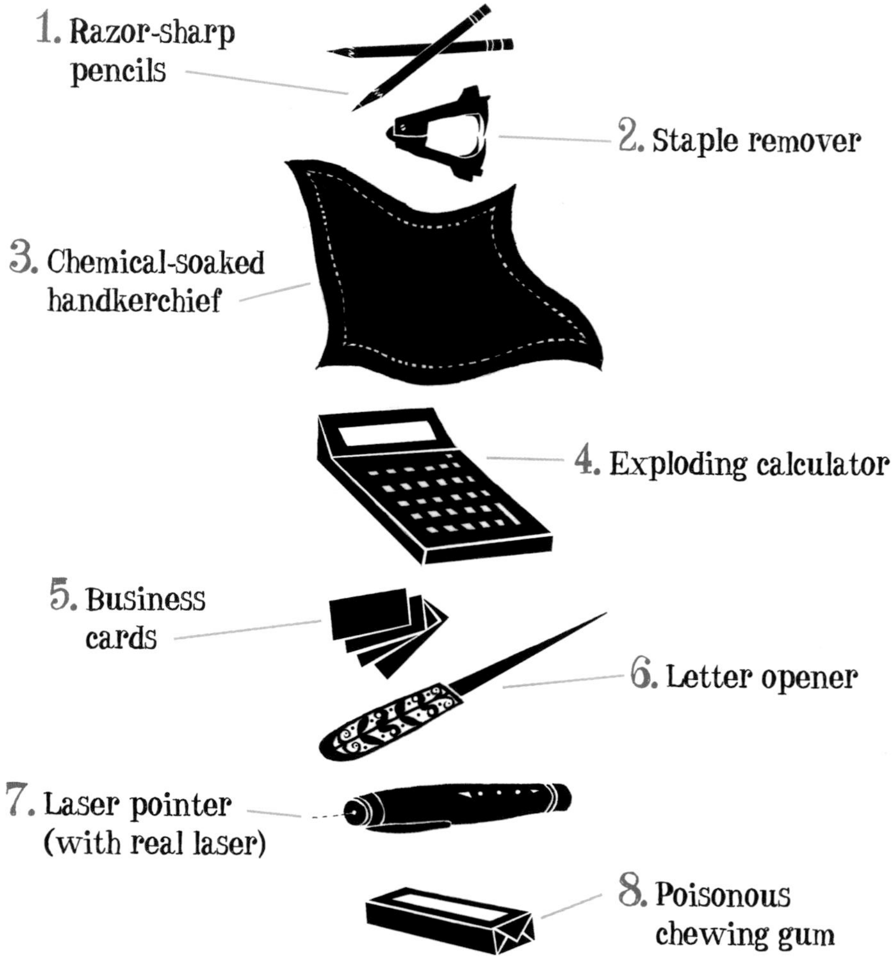

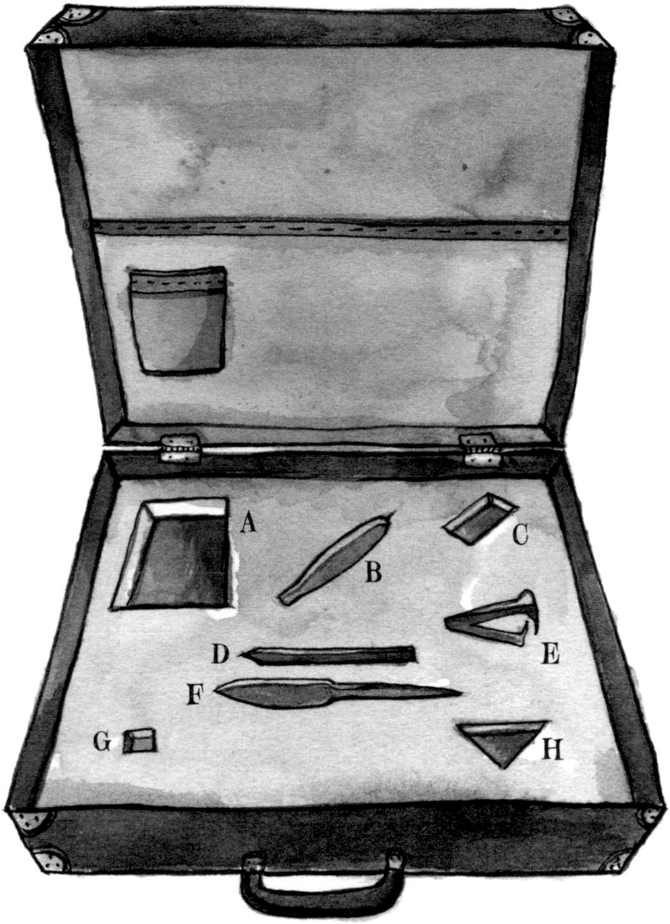


Pair the number of the item with its space within the briefcase.

A ____ B ____ C ____ D ____

E ____ F ____ G ____ H ____

# That's Far Enough

*It is very difficult to get close to someone like Mr. Curtain.*

It is exactly 11:45 AM, and Mr. Curtain
has caught up with you at last.
In fact, his wheelchair is now only sixty feet away
from where you are securely tied up.

Much to his chagrin, however, Mr. Curtain's wheelchair malfunctions. When he tries to move forward sixty feet, his wheelchair goes only half that far. Of course, this means he is now only thirty feet away. He zooms forward, but again only half as far as he would like . . . which means he is now merely fifteen feet from where you are a sitting duck.

In this manner, Mr. Curtain keeps lurching forward, each time getting closer. But with every lurch, he covers only half the distance that remains between you.

At what time will Mr. Curtain's
wheelchair crash into you?

_ ◯ _ _ _

"Oh, here's a clever one.
Do you remember this question from the first test? It reads, 'What is wrong with this statement?' And do you know what Constance wrote in reply? She wrote, 'What is wrong with *you*?' "

# CONTRARY *Indications*

*Written by Number Two, inspired by you know who*

After answering each of the questions on the opposite page, complete the instructions found above. (At last!)

_ _ _ _ _ _ _ _ _ _

_ _ _ _

1. Do you prefer being called short?
❍ Y ❍ N

2. Do you enjoy doing laundry?
❍ Y ❍ N

3. Do you admire the Ten Men?
❍ Y ❍ N

4. Would you like a headache?
❍ Y ❍ N

5. Isn't it lucky that Mr. Benedict has narcolepsy?
❍ Y ❍ N

6. Should we shake you when you fall asleep?
❍ Y ❍ N

7. Do you appreciate dishonesty?
❍ Y ❍ N

8. Isn't waiting fun?
❍ Y ❍ N

9. Would you describe Mr. Curtain as pleasant?
❍ Y ❍ N

10. Are you the most agreeable person on earth?
❍ Y ❍ N

11. Don't you think you've had enough sweets?
❍ Y ❍ N

12. Would you say you're fond of mildew?
❍ Y ❍ N

13. Would you like to answer more questions?
❍ Y ❍ N

# Rhyme Schemes and Far-Flung Plans

*Every poem is a maze, whose meaning is waiting to be found.*

**Begin with a G, then head straight to the end**  
There's **B** and there's **E**, now go find the script  
Which brings us to **O**, and from here to line two  
**I** is for you, and after **Z** there's just one  
*Add on the* L, *now for what you just skipped*  
**The last one is E, and now you are done.**  
The third letter is **T**, head to the line that is blue  
The next clue is **O**, now by one line ascend

_ _   _ _   _ _ O _ _ _

# Moocho's Perfect Pie

*Even the simplest of challenges sometimes confound us.*

Miss Perumal, her mother, Mr. Washington, Mrs. Washington, Ms. Plugg, Rhonda Kazembe, Number Two, Mr. Benedict, and Milligan would all very much like a piece of Moocho Brazo's famous apple pie.

Unfortunately, because Moocho ran out of eggs, he was able to bake only one pie today.

If you required only two pieces of pie, you could simply make a single cut down the middle. But if everyone who wants a piece is to enjoy one, what is the smallest number of cuts you must make?

O _ _ _

# Observations and COLD, HARD FACTS

*There is no place like home, especially for those of us who know what it is like not to have one.*

Mr. Benedict's house is very old. It has three floors plus a basement, each containing rambling hallways, a number of rooms, and quite a few nooks and crannies. Many walls have been knocked down and relocated over the years. (The first floor was, until recently, a maze, but it has since been converted into rooms.) The heating system in the house is inefficient, with the exception of the basement, which is climate-controlled. As a result, the third floor often feels like a furnace while the first floor feels like the opposite. Nearly every available surface in the house is covered with books. In fact, according to Sticky's calculations, there are exactly 120,136 volumes in the house. A number of reference books can be found on the third floor, including Greek, Latin, and Esperanto dictionaries. Number Two's bedroom is also on the third floor. A number of important books about narcolepsy can be found within Mr. Benedict's study on the second floor.

Nobody has been in the room on the opposite page in some time.

Which floor of the house is this room on?

**B 1 2 3**

THESAURUS
DICTIONARY
Encyclopedia
Encyclopedia
Encyclopedia
Encyclopedia
FRENCH
SPANISH

*This diagram, which still resides in government case files, was the result of our first opportunity to examine the Whisperer up close, after so many years of guessing at its construction. As you know, the device was modeled after my brother's brain, and originally responded only to his mental direction.*

**Executive brain amplifier**

Reads and converts electrical impulses and conscious directions originating in the cerebral cortex and frontal lobe of Mr. Curtain's brain

**Lobotomal coil**

Transmits impulses from Mr. Curtain's brain to that of the Messenger

**Mental collection basin**

Gathers messages for transmission to the public, using tidal turbine energy

**Transference helix**

Transmits thoughts from the brain of the Messenger to Mr. Curtain

**Restraining cuffs**

Increases the sense of control enjoyed by Mr. Curtain, and monitors pulse and vital signs of the Messenger

*We first became aware of Kate long before she responded to our advertisement in the newspaper. Indeed, we even attended the circus once and marveled at her agility.*

# Kate Wetherall

### Founding Member, The Mysterious Benedict Society

*Achievements* Conquered the Hoop of Fire while in the circus; faced down Ten Men on numerous occasions; almost never lost patience with Constance

*Expertise* Physical dexterity, enhanced by fearlessness

*Habits* Moving around

*History* Mother died when she was an infant; father disappeared when she was two; ran away to join the circus at age seven

*Family* Milligan, her father; Moocho Brazos, caregiver, baker, former circus performer, and friend; and her falcon, Madge (also known as Her Majesty the Queen)

It was a very old house, with gray stone walls, high arched windows, and a roof with red shingles that glowed like embers in the afternoon sun. Roses grew along the iron fence, and near the house towered a gigantic elm tree, perhaps older than the building itself, its green leaves tinged with the first yellows of autumn. Shaded by the elm's branches were an ivy-covered courtyard and the stone steps upon which they were to wait. The steps themselves were half-covered with ivy; they seemed an inviting place to rest.

# THE *Great Kate* WEATHER MACHINE

*Kate has been dreaming of doing something like this for a very long time. She even drew the pictures.*

Here are your supplies!

MARBLES 

 EXTRA-STRENGTH GLUE



ROPE 

 SLINGSHOT

MAGNET 

 WHISTLE (for summoning Madge, the falcon)

BUCKET

On the next page, you'll see how Kate's imagined run-in with the Ten Men began…and how it ended. After that, you'll see everything else that happened, but all jumbled up. It's your job to put the events on pages 45 to 47 in the right order, from 1 to 6. Write which item was used each time. Each item can be used only once, and one isn't used at all!



continued

Here's how it all began…
There she is!
Get her!

…And here's how it ended!

Place in order __________

Item used ______________

Place in order __________

Item used ______________

continued

Place in order __________
Item used ______________
I can't let go!
We're stuck!

Place in order __________
Item used ______________
It took my . . .
Come back here!

Place in order ________

Item used ________

Place in order ________

Item used ◯ ________

Kate seemed to have doubled in size. She had drawn back her broad shoulders and set her jaw, and something in her stance called to mind the contained ferocity of a lioness. But it was the fierceness in Kate's bright blue eyes that had the most striking effect. The sort of look that made you thankful she wasn't your enemy.

"It's not going to be over,"

Kate said firmly,

"until we *say* so."

# Mr. Curtain's CONTROLS

*We may never know the function of every button, lever, and pedal on my brother Ledroptha's wheelchair. But let us try.*

Off the coast of Scotland, there is an island with an abandoned village that you will surely recall. The following instructions were found near the grain silo.

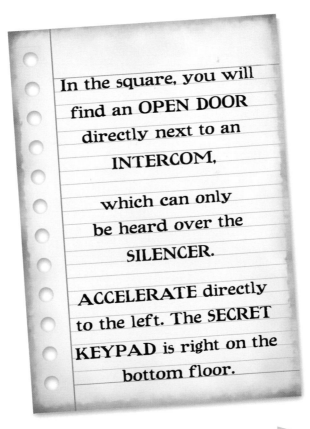

**In the square, you will find an OPEN DOOR directly next to an INTERCOM,**

**which can only be heard over the SILENCER.**

**ACCELERATE directly to the left. The SECRET KEYPAD is right on the bottom floor.**



continued

If this is the armrest of Mr. Curtain's wheelchair . . .

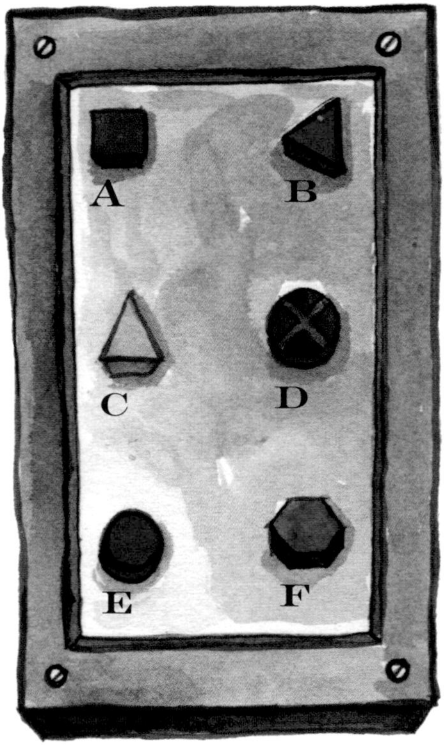


. . . which is the OFF button?

*We understood that L.I.V.E. operated according to its own rules, long before we had actually seen the rules themselves. This document was eventually recovered from the student dormitory by government agents.*

# L.I.V.E.

## The Learning Institute for the Very Enlightened

"Broadening the Minds of the Next Generation"

"At other academies, children are only taught how to survive. Reading skills, mathematics, art and music lessons — such a waste of a student's time! Here at the Learning Institute for the Very Enlightened, we show our students how to L.I.V.E.!"

— *Mr. Curtain, Founder of L.I.V.E.*

ACCEPTED

# RULES OF THE INSTITUTE

1. **There are no rules here!**
2. **You can wear whatever you like.** However, trousers, shoes, and shirts are required at all times. Messengers and Executives must wear their uniforms, including tunics and sashes.
3. **You don't have to bathe if you don't want to.** Simply be clean every day in class. When it comes to personal hygiene, there are unavoidable dangers that must be avoided at all costs.
4. **You may stay up as late at night as you wish.** Lights are turned off at 10:00 PM, and you must be in your room at that time.
5. **You are free to go where you please.** Please note, however, that you must keep to the paths and the yellow-tiled corridors. Also, leaving the grounds is not permitted at any time.
6. **Eat whatever you want, whenever you want.** Our Helpers are available to prepare your favorite delights. Meal hours are posted outside the cafeteria. Latecomers are not permitted.
7. **You will be called by the name you prefer.** Of course, nicknames are not tolerated unless they are official.
8. **Mr. Curtain and his actions are not to be questioned.**

# Constance Contraire

**FOUNDING MEMBER,**
**THE MYSTERIOUS BENEDICT SOCIETY**

*Achievements* Has never agreed to do anything

*Expertise* Poetic talent, coupled with extreme mental sensitivity

*Habits* Grumbling, protesting, demanding sweets, and napping

*History* Formerly lived in hiding in a storage room in the Brookville Library

*Family* Mr. Benedict, Rhonda Kazembe, and Number Two

*This page from one of Constance's notebooks provides insight into that rare pair of qualities that defines her: unruliness and poeticism.*

Loud Crowd

Old Mold

Lone Throne

Thin Skin

Hair Flair

Ancient Fungal blah blah

At least I'll have a ha ha ha

Wild Child

Brain Pain

Fake Quake

Bloom Room

Rock Jock

"Rules and schools
are tools for fools –
I don't give two mules
for rules!"

# STICKY'S Sweet

*A photographic memory lets nothing go unnoticed, as one of our favorite poems by Constance reminds us.*

## Why don't you leave? (Being a work in free verse)

BY CONSTANCE CONTRAIRE

O, why don't you leave?
It is winter and the flowers are gone, why do you not join them?
It is cold, all warmth has fled, why do you not follow it?
You speak and speak, the air is filled with your words,
But your words are meaningless —
Why not fill the air with youlessness instead?
I see you are angry about something I said.
I hear you say I have a problem.
But my problem is that I can see you and hear you,
For you have not gone, and will not go.

O, why do you not leave?
Why, when I insist that I wish to be left alone?
You say you will not leave until I give back your candy,
But how do you know the candy was not mine?
How do you know that I did not purchase it with my own money?
Why must you irk me with your questions and demands?
I wish to be alone!
We can discuss your candy later, after you have gone,
Just as your candy has gone. Yes, gone! For I have eaten it.
O, now you go? Now you leave, with a slamming of the door?
O, why did I not tell you before?

# BEFORE

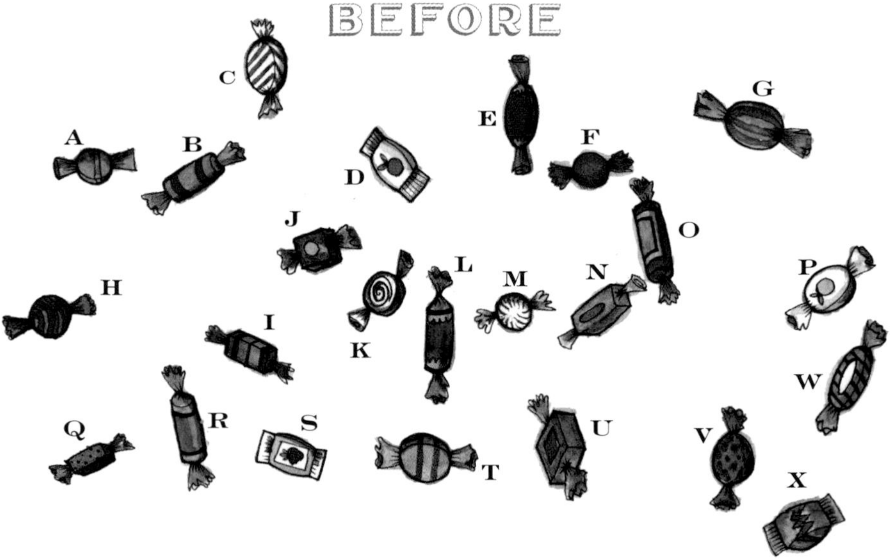


# AFTER

Which of Sticky's sweets did Constance swipe?

# Ducts and Decoys

*In light of Kate's particular affection for traveling through heating ducts, we decided to let this one squeeze through.*

By connecting only two of these ducts, you will be able to crawl from one room to the other. But which ducts are the ones that fit properly?

Circle the two ducts you need.

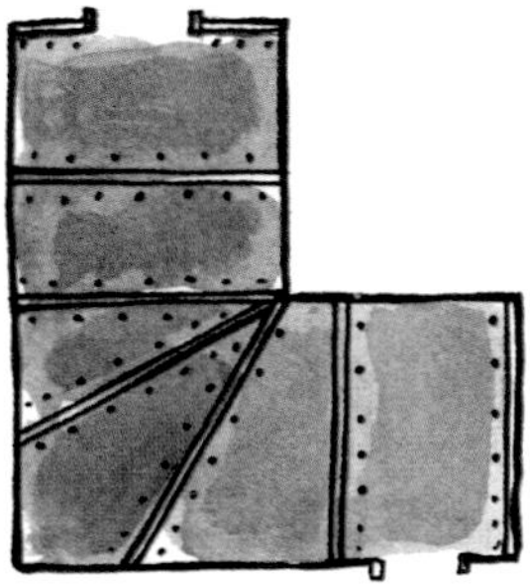

A.

B.

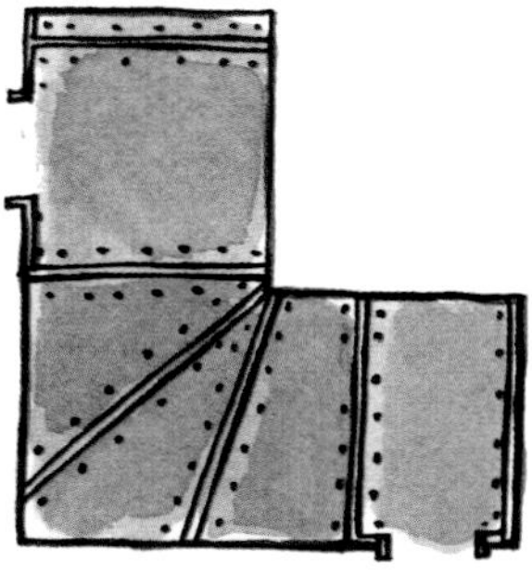

C.

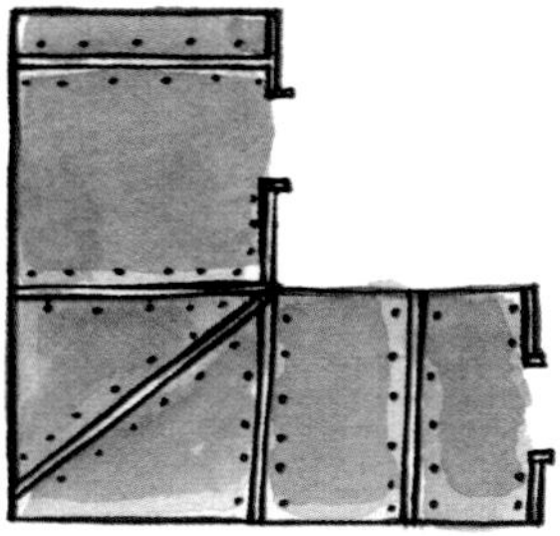

D.

# THREE Ways OUT

*When this appeared as part of the very first test, everyone failed to see the bigger picture — everyone, that is, except a girl dressed all in yellow. Her name was . . . well, let's just say it was Number Two.*

This room is completely empty and normal in every way.
You have nothing in your possession except
a small screwdriver.
There are exactly three ways out.
What are they?

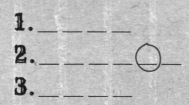

1. _ _ _ _
2. _ _ _ _ (_) _
3. _ _ _ _

# A
# *Is for* Apple

*If you think back, you may realize that you can recognize even the most complex of patterns in a matter of seconds.*

Number Two almost never sleeps, and because such wakefulness requires a great deal of energy, she is almost always eating. As a very orderly person, she has been known to follow a regimen that places special emphasis on what she eats, how often, and in what order.

Here is Number Two's record of what she ate in one twenty-four-hour period. Unfortunately, she was forced to violate her own dietary regimen exactly once during this period, due to an unavailability of ingredients at our local market.

Which food violated Number Two's regimen?

_ _ _ _ (_) _ _

# SUNDAY

12:07 AM zucchini sticks
12:53 AM yogurt
1:32 AM almonds
3:09 AM walnuts
4:22 AM vegetable smoothie
6:01 AM udon noodles
6:46 AM tuna salad
7:15 AM salami
8:07 AM rye bread with cheese
8:39 AM quiche
9:43 AM potato (baked)
9:59 AM orange
10:32 AM nachos
12:01 PM muffin
12:47 PM lamb chop
1:36 PM kumquats
2:54 PM jam and toast
3:40 PM ice cream
5:23 PM halibut
6:19 PM grapes
6:58 PM French onion soup
7:18 PM egg (hard boiled)
8:35 PM dandelion salad
9:15 PM crackers
9:37 PM banana
11:56 PM apple

"There are tests,"
said Mr. Benedict,
"and then there are tests."

*When I first received this telegram regarding a now-infamous encounter with several Ten Men,
I laughed so hard that I immediately fell asleep.*

# TELEGRAM

MISSION TO INTERCEPT TEN MEN
SUCCESSFUL STOP DISGUISED MYSELF
AS JANITOR AT KAKUTO LABORATORY
STOP THIRTY THREE PENCILS EVADED
STOP ONE MOP DISCHARGED STOP
APOLOGIES TO JANITOR FOR THE
MESS STOP

# Milligan

**SPECIAL AGENT**

*Achievements* Evaded 873 pencils in the line of duty; saved the lives of the Mysterious Benedict Society members on more than one occasion; has never done another person irreparable bodily harm

*Expertise* Master of disguise; extraordinary mental and physical fortitude and creativity

*History* Captured on a mission more than ten years ago and suffered near-total amnesia; went to work for Mr. Benedict after escaping captors; regained memory in final hours on Nomansan Island, including recognizing his daughter

# Finding MILLIGAN

*Even when we did not know exactly who Milligan was, we knew what he was made of. This challenge was designed by Reynie in his honor.*

Amid all the finger-pointing
Find the Milligan you can trust
Though he hides among the crowd
His sentries are equally just

Once you have found Milligan, enter his location.

__ ◯



continued

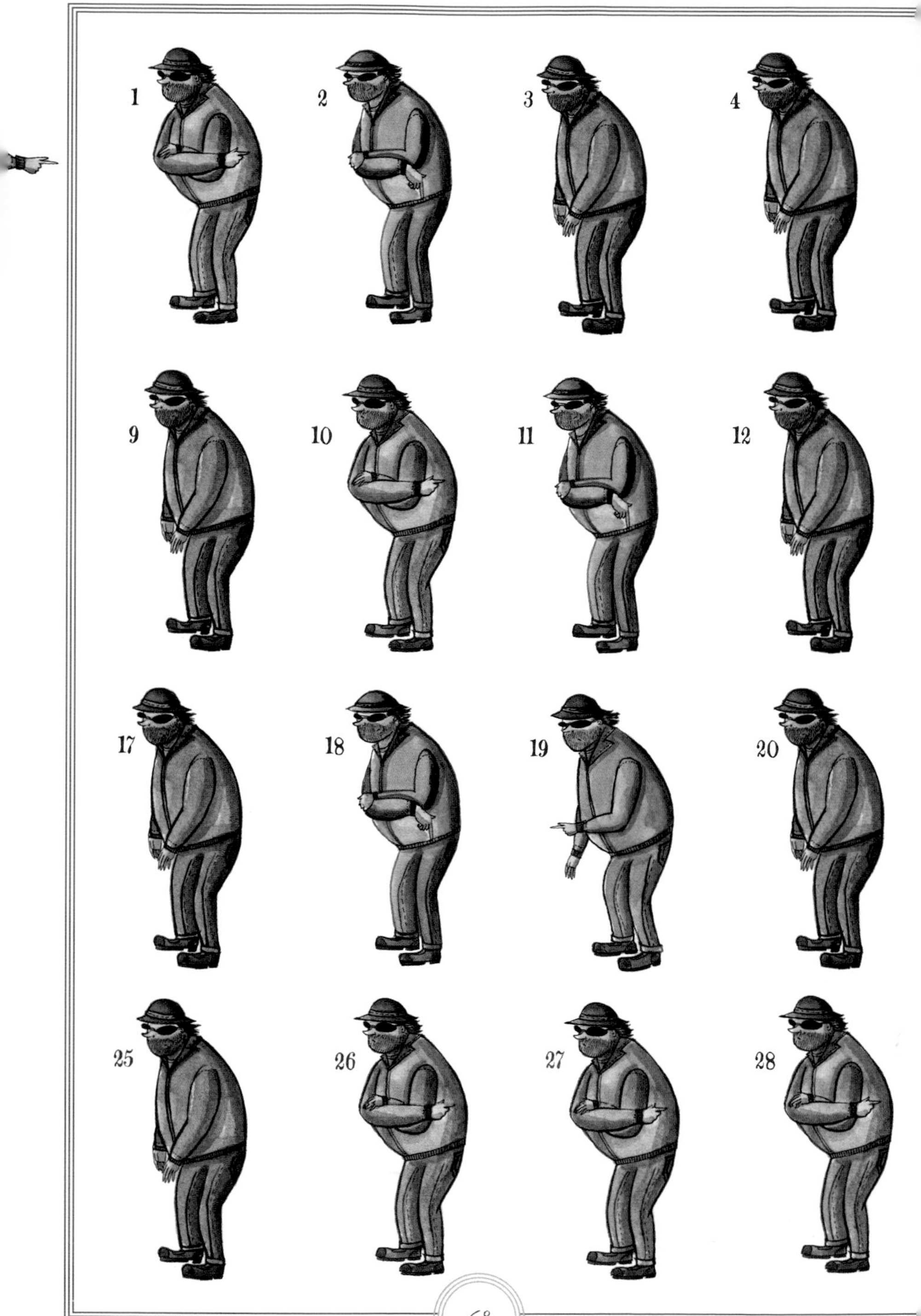
1
2
3
4
9
10
11
12
17
18
19
20
25
26
27
28

5

6

7

8

13

14

15

16

21

22

23

24

29

30

31

32

continued

33
34
35
36
37
38
39
40
41
42
43
44
45
46
47
48

"Will this test be any harder than the last one?" Kate asked, with a show of bravado.

"Some find it quite difficult," said Rhonda. "But you should all be able to do it with your eyes closed."

"Will it be scary?" Sticky asked, almost in a whisper.

"Maybe, but it isn't really dangerous," Rhonda said, which did nothing for Sticky's confidence.

"Who goes first?" Reynie asked.

"That's an easy one," Rhonda answered. "You."

# S.Q.'s Vocabulization

*We must never give up on the S.Q.'s of the world, whose good natures sometimes lead them to do that which they do not mean.*

S.Q. is often confused.
In fact, he routinely mangles his words.

For each sentence spoken by S.Q., can you figure out what two similar words he might possibly mean?

1. "I'm simply astoundished!"

a_____________d a_____________d

2. "Let's inspectigate!"

i_____________t i_____________e

3. "That seems very complexicated."

c_____________x c_____________d

4. "How infuritating!"

i_____________g i_____________g

5. "This is most unsuitisfactory."

u_____________e u_____________y

6. "I'm very disperturbed."

d_____________d p_____________d

7. "Mr. Curtain is quite innoventive."

i_____________e i_____________e

8. "This is cataclystrophic!"

c_____________c c_____________c

9. "I find such behavior repellsive."

r_____________t r_____________e

10. "I'm baffuddled."

b_____________d b_____________d

*After his departure from the Navy, Captain Noland sent this brochure to inform us of his new position. As he wrote in an accompanying note, "No ship loads and unloads faster, and thus spends less time in port — a dream come true for me!" The brochure's headline became the inspiration for a hidden code that led to the ship.*

# TAKE THE *SHORTCUT!*

## THE SPEEDIEST CARGO SHIP *IN HISTORY*

FIVE TIMES AS FAST AS ANY IN ITS CLASS

CAN CROSS THE ATLANTIC IN TWO DAYS FLAT!

*The MV* Shortcut *is*

# A FEAT OF MODERN NAVAL AND COMMERCIAL TECHNOLOGY,

*its every detail designed with speed in mind.*

- Hydrodynamic hull design reduces resistance on the water by over 30 percent.
- Jet propulsion system efficiently produces speeds upward of 60 knots.
- Patented "Cargo-to-Go" system means containers can be rolled on and off in a fraction of the time normally required.

*The MV* Shortcut *is not just the fastest way, it's also the most secure, with a high-security cargo hold designed by world-renowned vault designer Hans Warrilow. Large enough to hold the ship's entire crew, constructed of three-foot-thick expanded metal, and lockable from the inside in case of attack, nothing could keep your precious cargo safer.*

## CAPTAIN PHILIP NOLAND AND HIS CREW

INVITE YOUR CARGO TO JOIN THE MV *SHORTCUT*'S MAIDEN TWO-DAY ATLANTIC CROSSING FROM STONETOWN HARBOR TO

THE PORT OF LISBON, PORTUGAL.

DEPARTING AT 4:00 PM

**September 19**

# GOVERNMENT DOSSIER

# THE TEN MEN

### WHO ARE THEY?

The Ten Men are well-dressed professionals who do Mr. Curtain's dirty work. They were previously known as Recruiters, due to their role in "recruiting" — often just another word for kidnapping — orphans and runaways to bring to the Learning Institute for the Very Enlightened.

---

### WHY ARE THEY DANGEROUS?

The Ten Men are believed to have ten ways of hurting their victims — thus, their name. Many of their weapons are thought to have been designed by Mr. Curtain himself. Each Ten Man carries a briefcase containing an arsenal of dangerous supplies: razor-sharp pencils, poisonous chewing gum, a laser pointer that fires a real laser, and so on.

---

### HOW CAN THEY BE IDENTIFIED?

Since they dress like common businessmen, the Ten Men frequently go undetected. However, one identifying feature is the presence of shockwatches — dangerous accessories that emit wires capable of electrifying their victims — on both wrists. Another is their eerily calm behavior. Some Ten Men have been known to speak to their intended victims in childish barnyard terms, such as "Ducky" or "Chickie."

McCracken
Crawlings
Garrotte
Sharpe

# Salamander *vs.* WHISPERER

*Kate has an uncommon knack for calculating distances and other spatial relationships — but even those without her gifts can bounce back.*

Near a high reflective wall, you succeed in taking control of Mr. Curtain's Salamander and discover that it has been modified with a special transmitter. This transmitter emits a spherical energy field capable of disabling any electrical device.

Your mission is to disable the Whisperer, which is positioned nearby.

Where should you aim the transmitter on the reflective wall in order to disable the Whisperer?

______

-2
-1
0
1
2

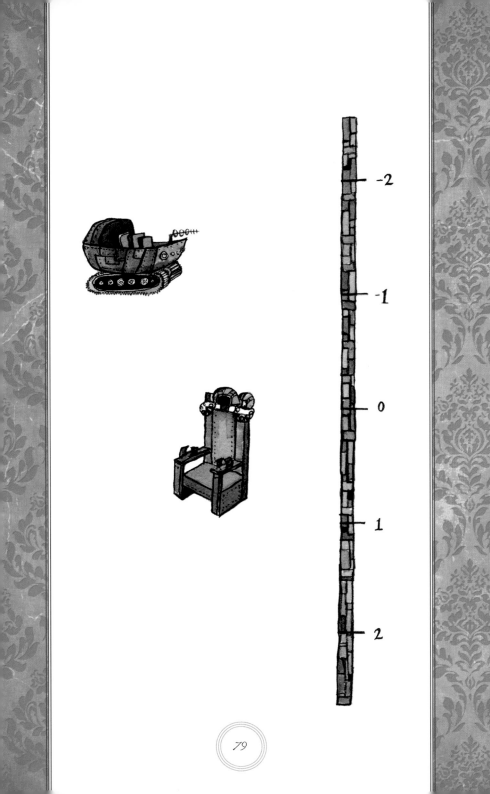

# Madge's Bird's-Eye View

*Few skills are more valuable than the ability to see things from an entirely different perspective.*

Circling high overhead, Kate's falcon, Madge, spies this scene far below.

Where is Kate?

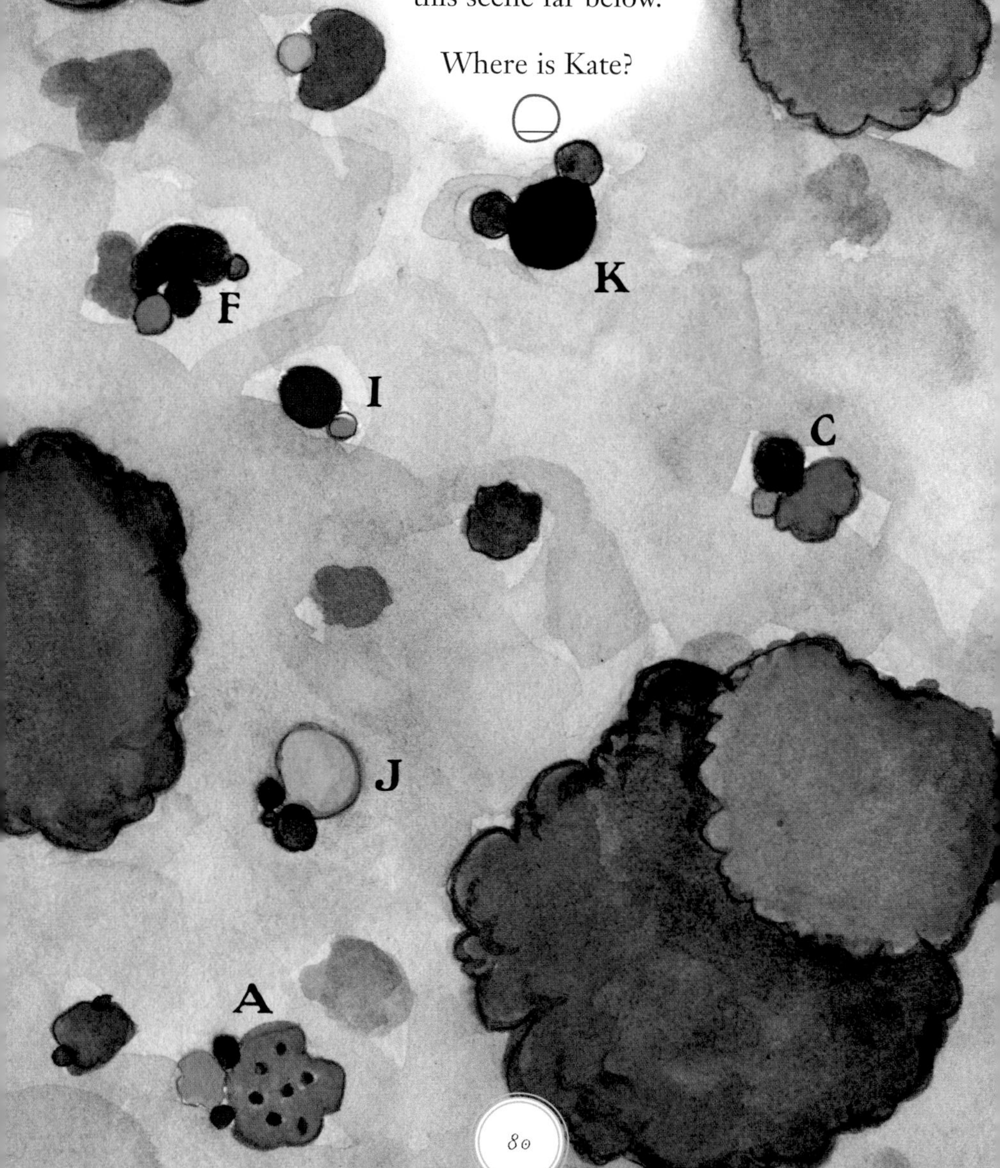

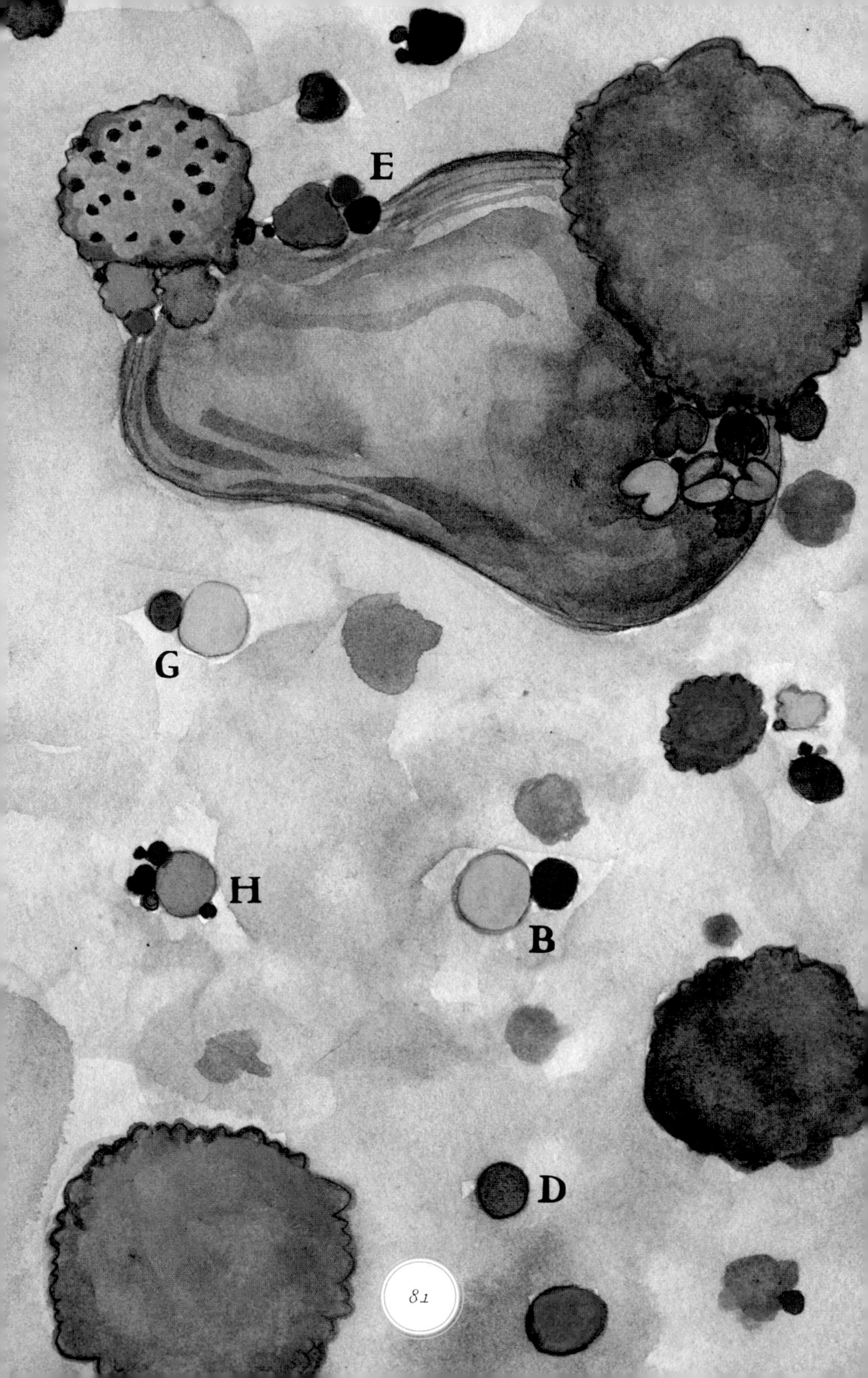
E
G
H
B
D

# Rare Pair

*Only someone of Constance's temperament could reduce an entire impenetrable book into two amusing words that rhyme.*

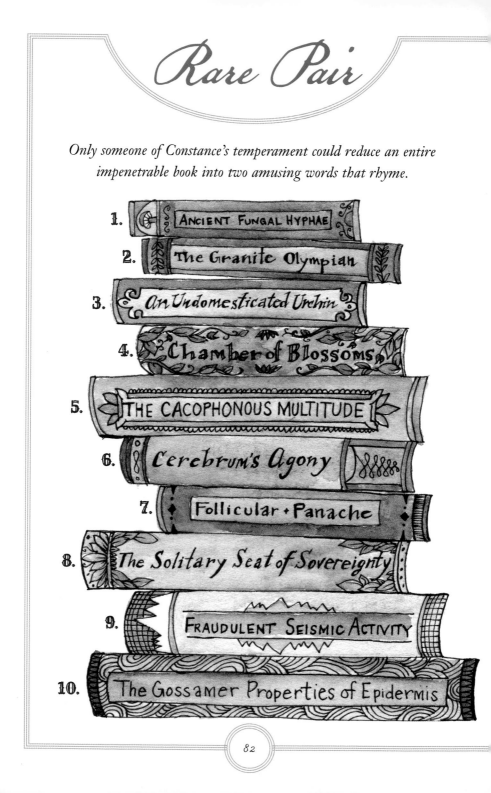

Sticky once attempted to explain to Constance just a few of the 1,737 books found in Mr. Benedict's study. It pleased him greatly when she appeared to be taking studious notes.

However, when at last Constance revealed what she'd been writing, he saw that she had turned each title into nothing more than two rhyming words.

Like Constance, translate each book's title into a pair of amusing one-syllable words that rhyme.

1. _ _ _   _ _ _ _

2. _ _ _ _   _ _ _ _

3. _ _ _ _   _ _ _ _ _

4. _ _ _ _ _   _ _ _ _

5. _ _ _ _   _ _ _ _ _

6. _ _ _ _ _   _ _ _ _

7. _ _ _ _   _ _ _ _ _

8. _ _ _ _   _ _ _ _ _ (_)

9. _ _ _ _   _ _ _ _ _

10. _ _ _ _   _ _ _ _

Together, privately, the children thought of themselves as the Mysterious Benedict Society, and as such they had held a great many meetings — some in extraordinarily dire circumstances.

# Tamil
# SQUARES

*Miss Perumal used these simple puzzles from her childhood to teach Reynie how to think in Tamil, her native tongue. Now it's your turn.*

A complete Tamil square includes all of the numbers 1 through 9. (If you are unfamiliar with Tamil numbers, please consult the Helpful Resources.)

Solve each Tamil square by filling in the missing numeral in the middle. The first has been done for you.



continued

| | | |
|---|---|---|
| ௪ | ௫ | ௮ |
| ௩ | ௭ | ௧ |
| ௨ | ௯ | ௬ |

| | | |
|---|---|---|
| ௭ | ௬ | ௧ |
| ௨ | | ௩ |
| ௯ | ௫ | ௮ |

| | | |
|---|---|---|
| ௧ | ௩ | ௪ |
| ௮ | | ௯ |
| ௭ | ௬ | ௫ |

| | | |
|---|---|---|
| ௨ | ௬ | ௭ |
| ௫ | | ௮ |
| ௯ | ௩ | ௪ |

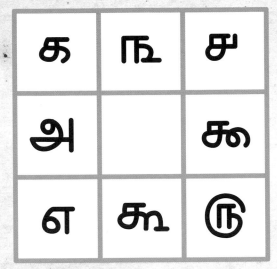

continued

| | | |
|---|---|---|
| ௬ | ௪ | ௮ |
| ௧ | | ௭ |
| ௩ | ௨ | ௯ |

| | | |
|---|---|---|
| ௫ | ௬ | ௨ |
| ௩ | | ௧ |
| ௪ | ௭ | ௮ |

# Jackson *and* Jillson's NURSERY RHYME

*Executives who are obstructive can be very instructive.*

Jackson and Jillson went up the hillson

To fetchet a pailet of water.

Jackson fell downdown and brokedown
his crowndown

And Jillson came trampleson after.

What is the correct spelling of the misspelled word?

(__) __ __ __ __ __ __ __ __ __ __

# Shortcuts *and* Sudden Turns

*This gem comes from our old friend Cannonball!*

Cut through the clutter
Then meet in the gutter
The bullfrog will shudder
To lose his bread and butter!

What did you find?

__ __ ◯ __ __ __ __

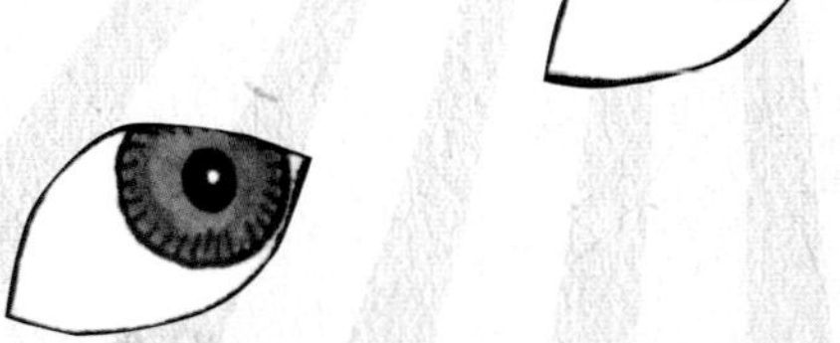

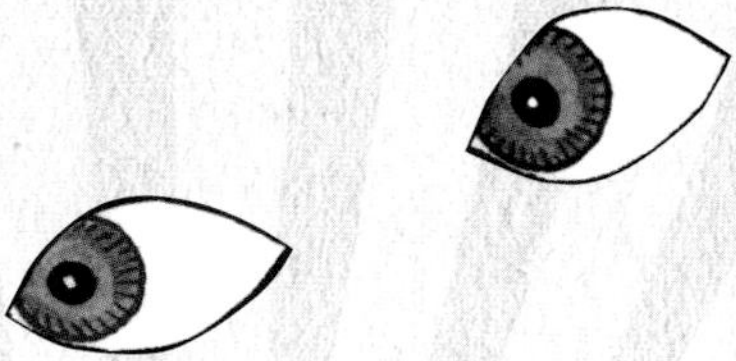

CLUTTERTCLUTTERUCLUTTERRCLUTTE
RNCLUTTERTCLUTTERHCLUTTERECLUT
TERCCLUTTEROCLUTTERRCLUTTERNCL
UTTERECLUTTERRCLUTTERS

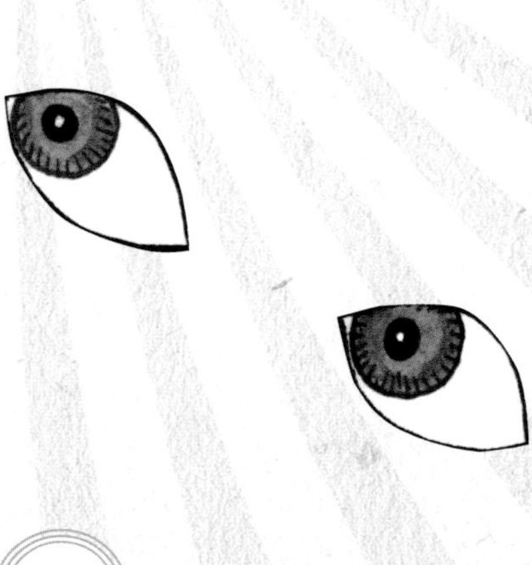

# THE
# Table of Contents

*See the Table of Contents.*

In a book like this, the Table of Contents
tells you where to go.

It lists proper names and page numbers.

It appears before the beginning but after the title.

And it's really quite simple to use.

What's found in the Table of Contents?

__ __ (__) __ __ __

# UNIDENTICAL TWINS

*Our most basic assumptions sometimes mislead us.*

A kindhearted genius had a long-lost twin brother who was an inventor.

What relation was the kindhearted genius to the brother who was an inventor?

__ __ __ __ (__) __

# Through THE LOOKING GLASS

*Upon reflection, the solution may be right in front of you.*

You are a spy at Mr. Curtain's Learning Institute for the Very Enlightened (L.I.V.E.), and you have been caught. In fact, a mob of Executives is now chasing you through the halls of the student dormitory.

Milligan appears suddenly from a student washroom and pulls you inside. By the sink, he thrusts a piece of paper into your hand and says, "I'll hold them off while you escape," before disappearing back into the hallway.

Here is the piece of paper.

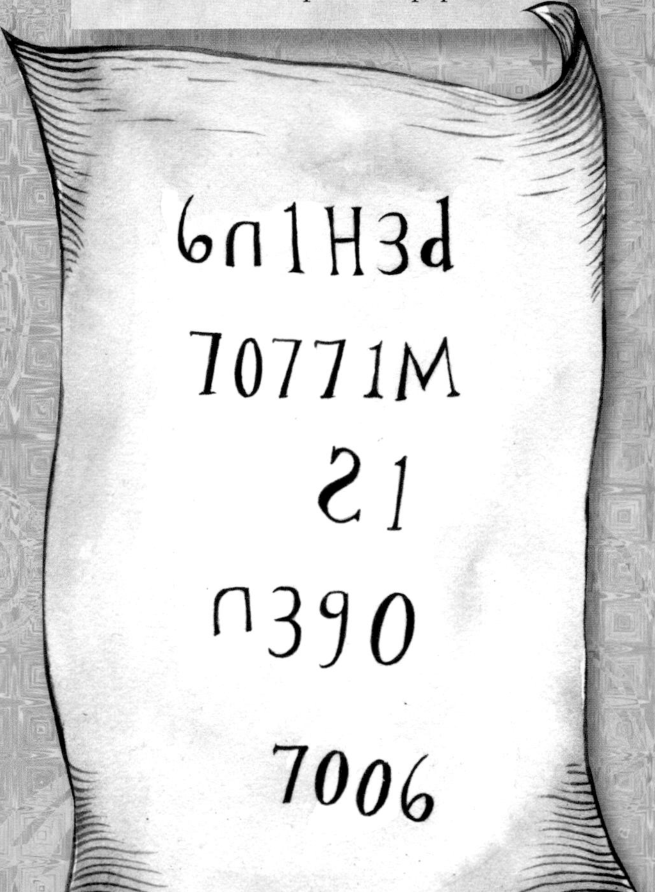


Where is the secret door?

__ __ __ __ __ __ the __ __ __ __ __ __ __

LEARNING INSTITUTE
FOR THE
VERY ENLIGHTENED

# GOVERNMENT DOSSIER

## LEDROPTHA CURTAIN

### WHO IS HE?

Mr. Curtain is the founder of the Learning Institute for the Very Enlightened (L.I.V.E.), a secluded boarding school now known to be the source of telepathic transmissions during the Emergency. In addition to inventing the Whisperer, a highly advanced machine capable of mind control, Mr. Curtain has been responsible for a series of significant scientific breakthroughs, including tidal turbine energy and mobile noise cancellation. Unfortunately, he appears determined to use his genius for nefarious purposes.

### WHAT DOES HE WANT?

In a word, control. Ledroptha Curtain has hatched one bold plan after another in hopes of seizing power over the global population. His grand mind-control scheme, code-named "the Improvement," would have affected billions — as would his quest to acquire the fabled plant known as duskwort, which is allegedly capable of putting anyone to sleep.

### HOW CAN HE BE IDENTIFIED?

With some difficulty, because Mr. Curtain is now known to have an identical twin: the brilliant Nicholas Benedict. Notably, however, Mr. Curtain almost always wears mirrored sunglasses and travels in a specially equipped wheelchair in order to hide his narcoleptic condition.

*Fortunately, my brother, Ledroptha, never had a chance to use the pamphlets discovered on Nomansan Island. But did you notice what the title he hoped to bestow upon himself really stood for?*

# OFFICIAL ADVISORY

## of the Public Health Administration

## SUDDEN AMNESIA DISEASE

**Just what *is* Sudden Amnesia Disease (SAD)?** SAD is an extremely contagious disease that causes total memory loss in those who contract it.

**What's being done about it?** Although the origin and cure of this disease have yet to be found, they're being investigated by a group of experts headed by none other than Ledroptha Curtain, the highly regarded scientist and our newly named Minister And Secretary of all The Earth's Regions. SAD cases are admitted for free care at the Amnesia Sanctuary on Nomansan Island, a state-of-the-art facility where patients live comfortably, under strict quarantine, while the cure for their disease is sought.

**Am *I* a SAD case? Are my neighbors?** A common first symptom of SAD is the belief that one hears children's voices in one's head. The onset of this symptom is most sudden, and once it has begun, it persists without interruption until amnesia sets in.

*Already feeling better!*
*A SAD case jokes around with our friendly doctors.*

"As it so happens, however, I now find myself in the presence of the best possible team of children I could ever hope for — indeed, have long hoped for — and with not a minute to lose. In other words, you are our last possible hope. You are our *only* hope."

# WELCOME TO MEMORY TERMINAL

*Challenges like this, which require you to "spot the difference," were favored by Number Two when she was younger. They provide an exceedingly simple and effective method for honing one's observation skills.*

The Memory Terminal is filled with hundreds of machines called Sweepers. As part of Mr. Curtain's plan for the Improvement, these machines are to be used to bury the memories of millions around the globe.

However, the key to his entire plan is the Whisperer, a far more sophisticated, one-of-a-kind, delicately balanced invention that responds only to Mr. Curtain's strict mental direction. But in a sea of Sweepers, how can you tell which is the Whisperer?

Consider the next two pages.

Which one is the Whisperer?



continued

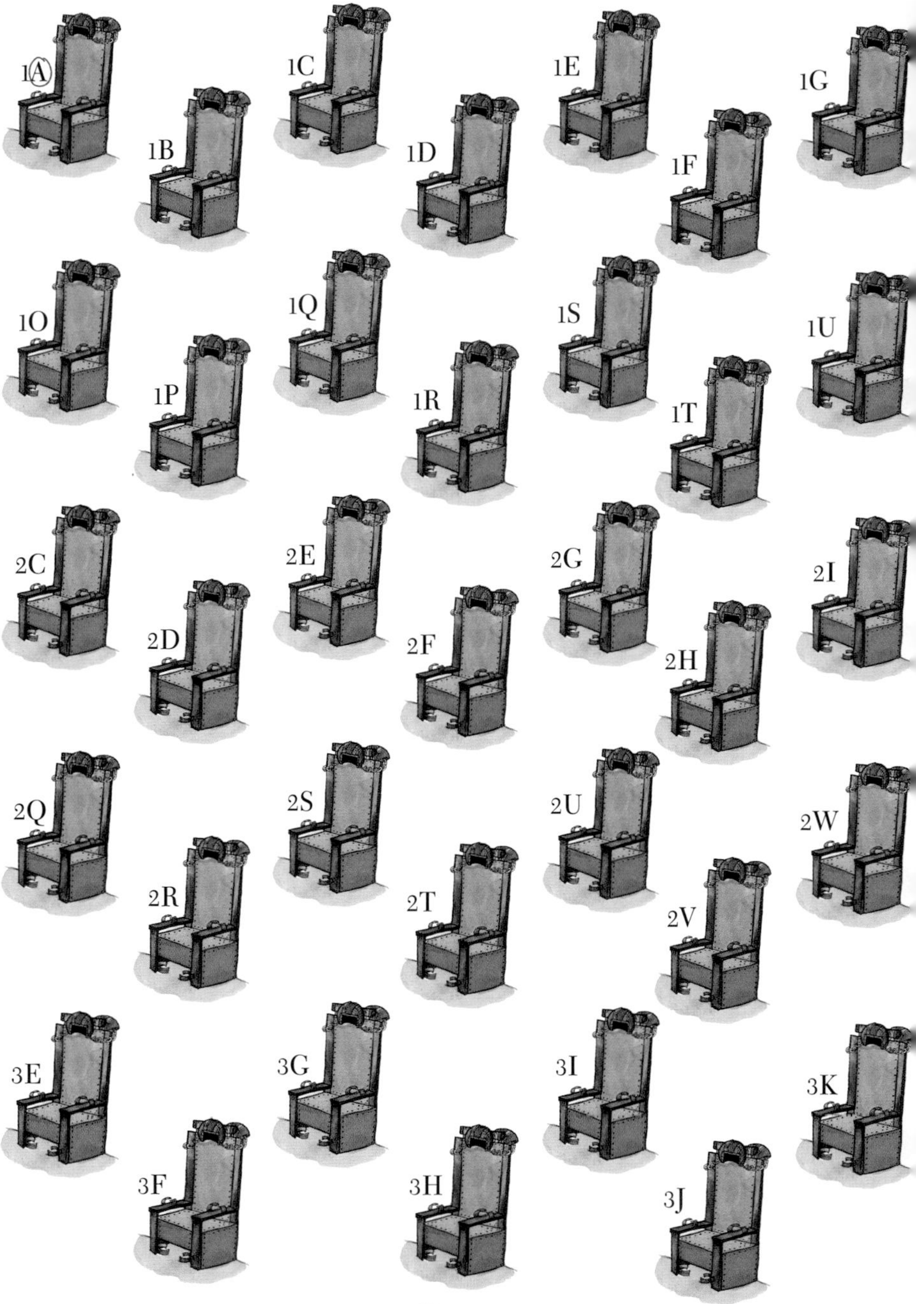
1A
1B
1C
1D
1E
1F
1G
1O
1P
1Q
1R
1S
1T
1U
2C
2D
2E
2F
2G
2H
2I
2Q
2R
2S
2T
2U
2V
2W
3E
3F
3G
3H
3I
3J
3K

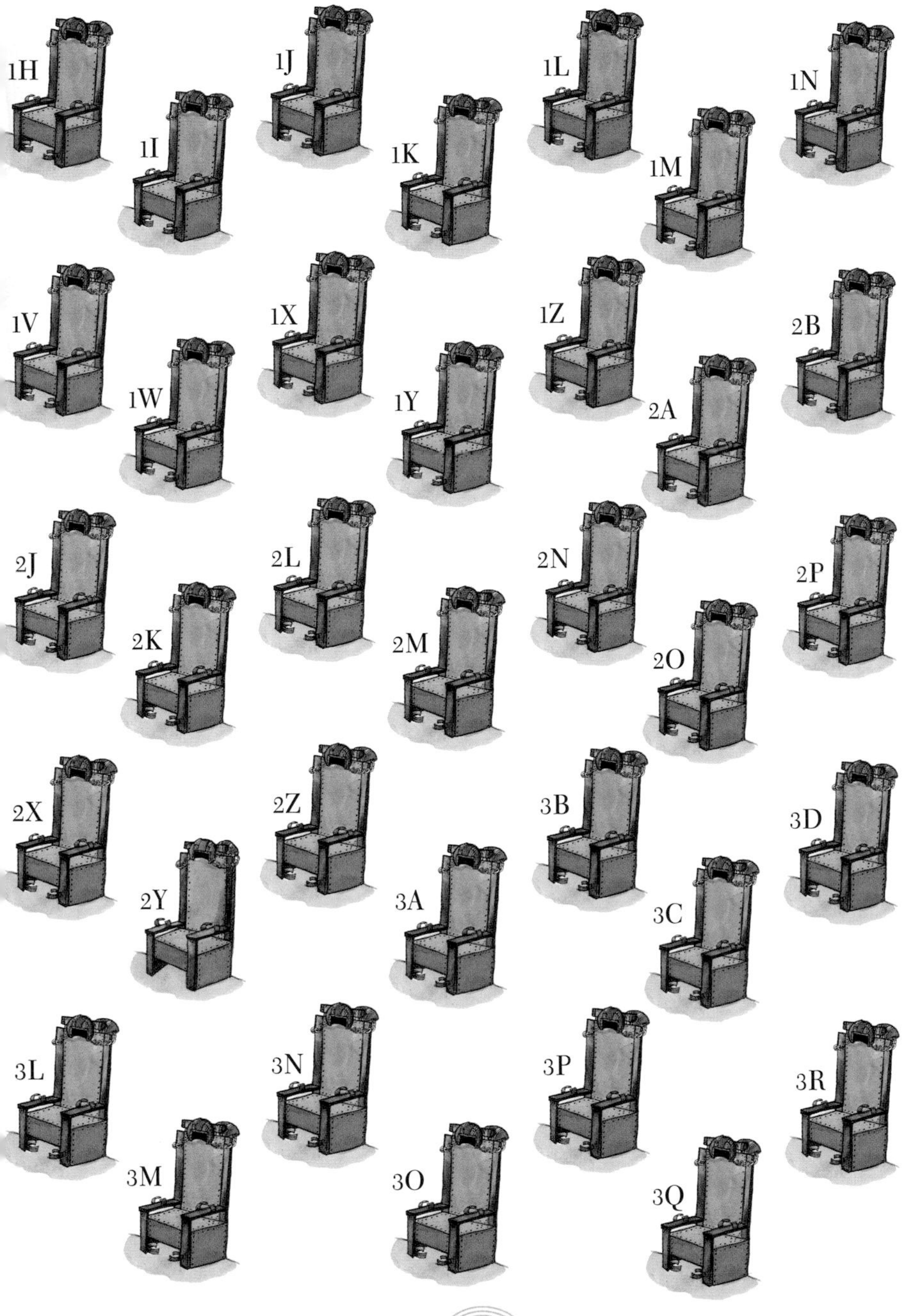
1H
1I
1J
1K
1L
1M
1N
1V
1W
1X
1Y
1Z
2A
2B
2J
2K
2L
2M
2N
2O
2P
2X
2Y
2Z
3A
3B
3C
3D
3L
3M
3N
3O
3P
3Q
3R

# SIX Buckets

*Reynie conceived this challenge while pacing in his room, inspired by Kate's red bucket before it was modified with a flip-top. Let us see how your thinking stacks up.*

Six buckets are arranged before you,
as seen on the opposite page.

How can you make two lines, each with four buckets,
by moving only one bucket?

Which bucket will you move?

_____

To which position?

_____

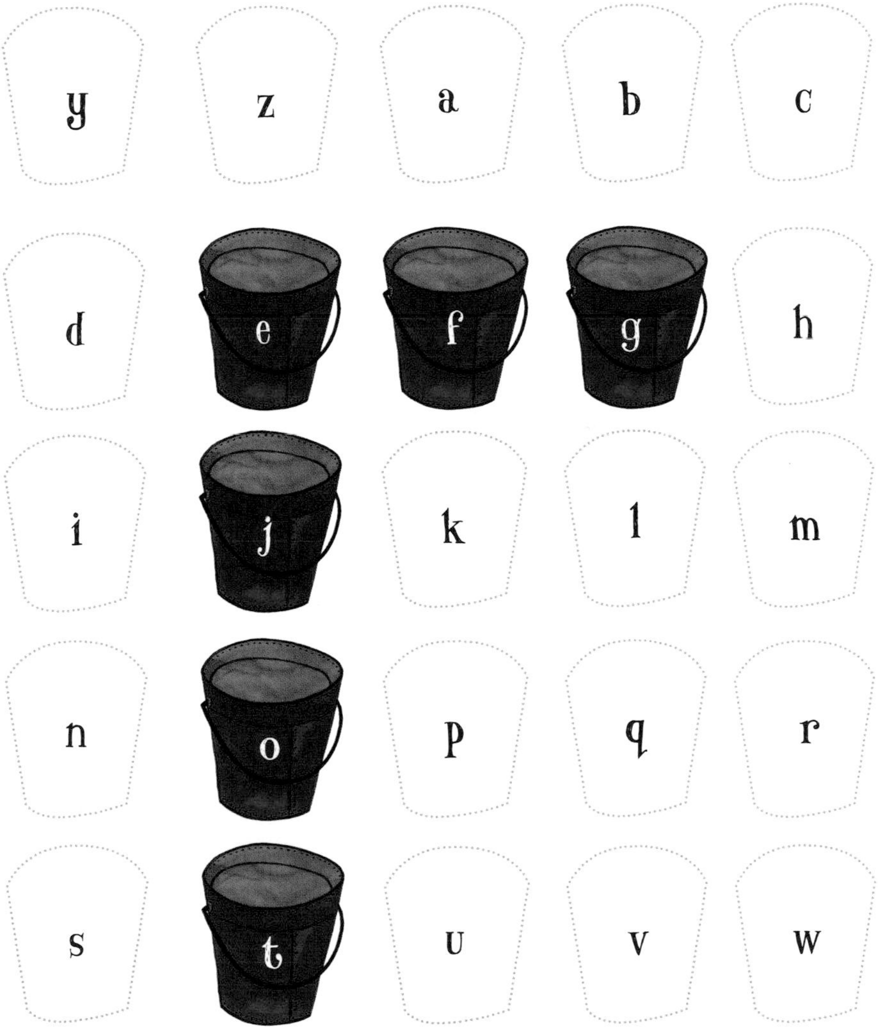
y
z
a
b
c
d
e
f
g
h
i
j
k
l
m
n
o
p
q
r
s
t
u
v
w

# Limericks *and* Accusations

*Initially, you might find little worth reading in Constance's poetry — but then you grow to appreciate her mischievous sense of humor.*

(This exercise was the result of an assignment given to Constance as part of her lessons. It is reprinted here without permission.)

## 1.

**There once was a sturgeon named Sticky,**
**Whose scales were all slimy and icky.**
**A most nasty fish,**
**But I got my wish,**
**And wishers must never be picky!**

## 2.

There once was an ingrate named Kate,
Who disliked what was put on her plate,
Just because I had taken
Every bit of her bacon
And replaced it with peas, which I hate!

## 3.

Now here is a blockhead named Reynie.
Often he secretly thinks I am whiny.
Tonight I shall sneak to his bed,
Mess not with his mind but his head.
Even to Sticky, his scalp will seem shiny!

Which one of these limericks was clearly NOT written by Constance Contraire?

______

# Rhonda Kazembe

**ASSOCIATE TO MR. BENEDICT**

*Achievements* Trained the members of the Mysterious Benedict Society; faithfully supported Mr. Benedict in all of his endeavors

*Expertise* Varied, with a memory nearly as good as Sticky's and a very even temperament

*History* Born in Zambia; brought to Stonetown as a child

# Recollections *and* Lucky Predictions

*This was one of the first exercises Rhonda ever created herself, shortly after beginning her studies with us.*

Before turning the page, study this number carefully. Perhaps you will find it easy to memorize.

continued

Without referring to the previous page, complete the number below.

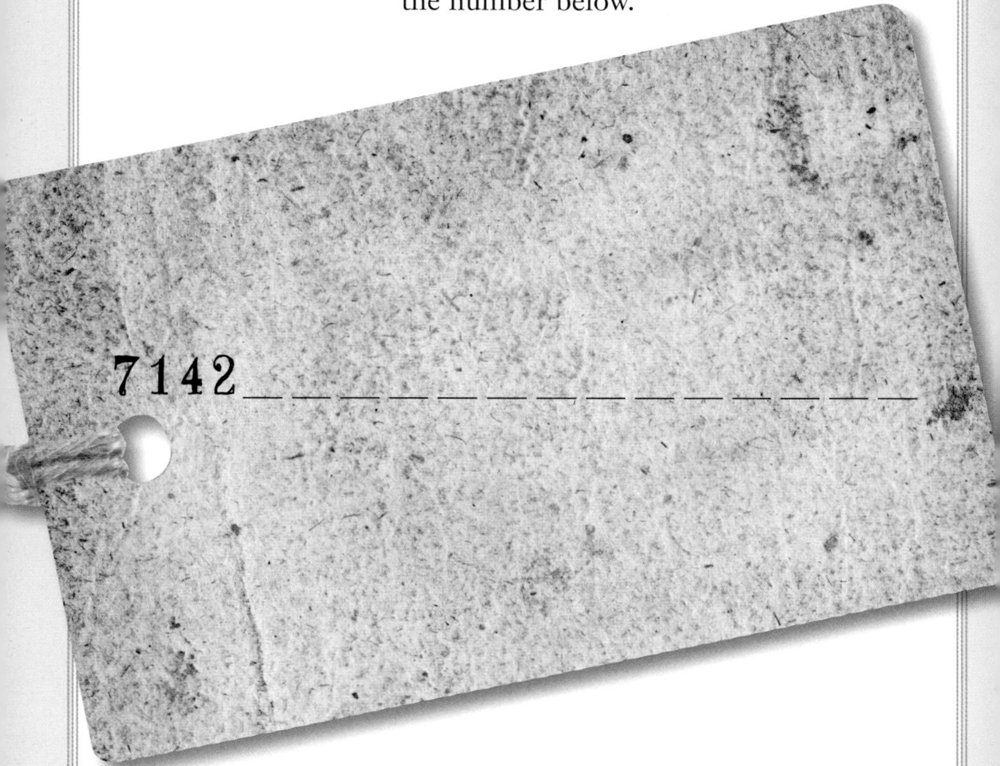


What is the nineteenth number in the sequence?

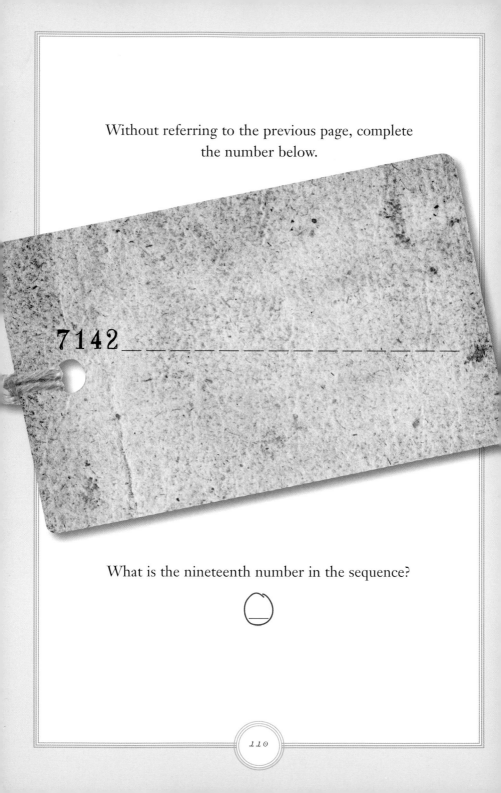

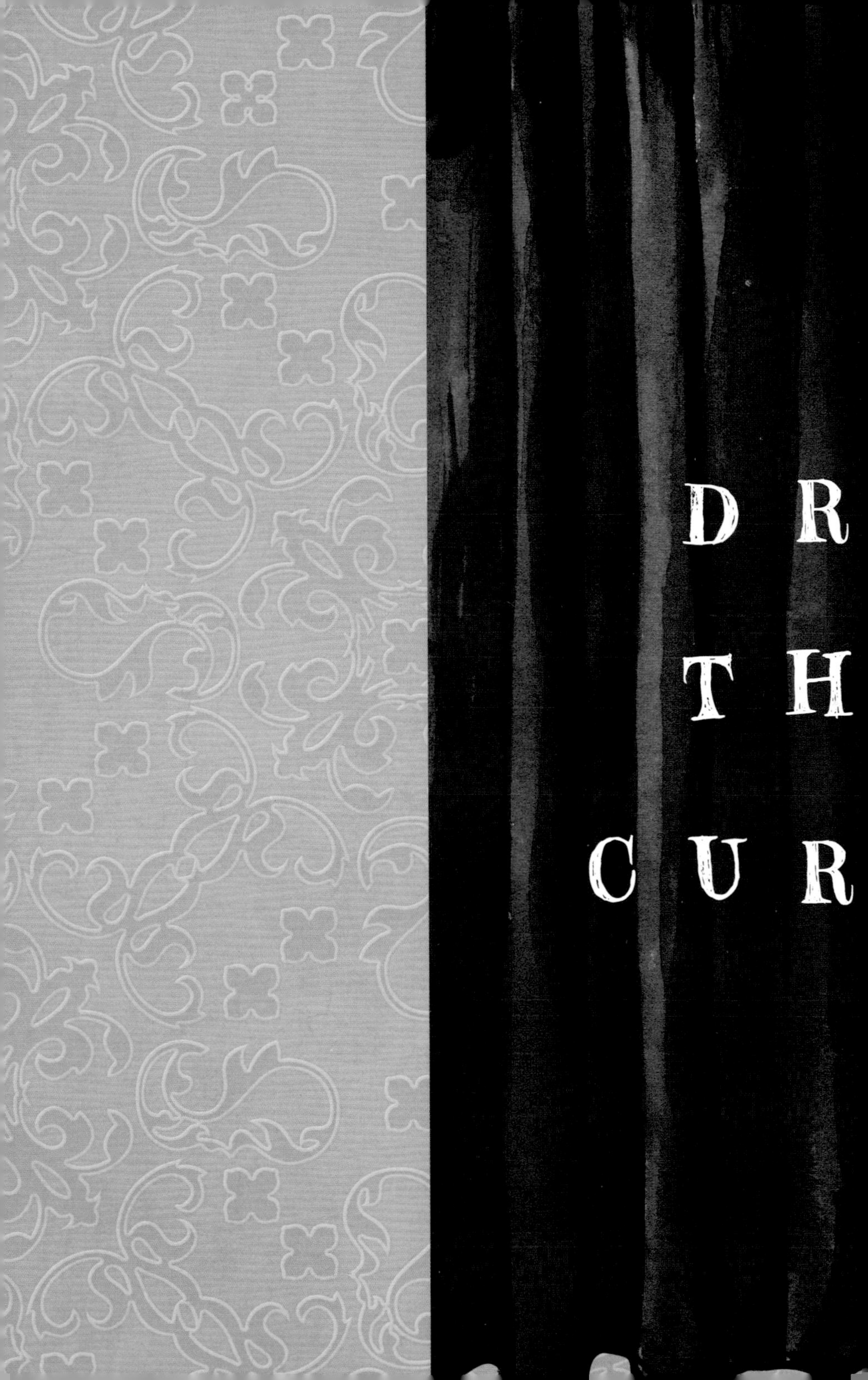
DR
TH
CUR

# The Show Must Not Go On

*Whenever someone gets in a flap,*
*turn it to your advantage.*

Mr. Curtain's Executive Martina Crowe has decided to lecture you about how much she dislikes you, as well as other things she hates. Because she hates so many things, it promises to be a very long and tedious lecture, and she has procured a magnificent theater for the occasion, using proceeds from Mr. Pressius's diamond scam.

What is the quickest way to end
Martina's lecture?
__ __ __ __   __ __ __
__ __ __ __ __ __ __

A W
E
T A I N

# PROCESSES and ELIMINATIONS

*Few people notice everything. Fewer still notice what is missing.*

One person compiled the personal profiles found throughout this book.
Which of the following people was it?
Enter the number below.

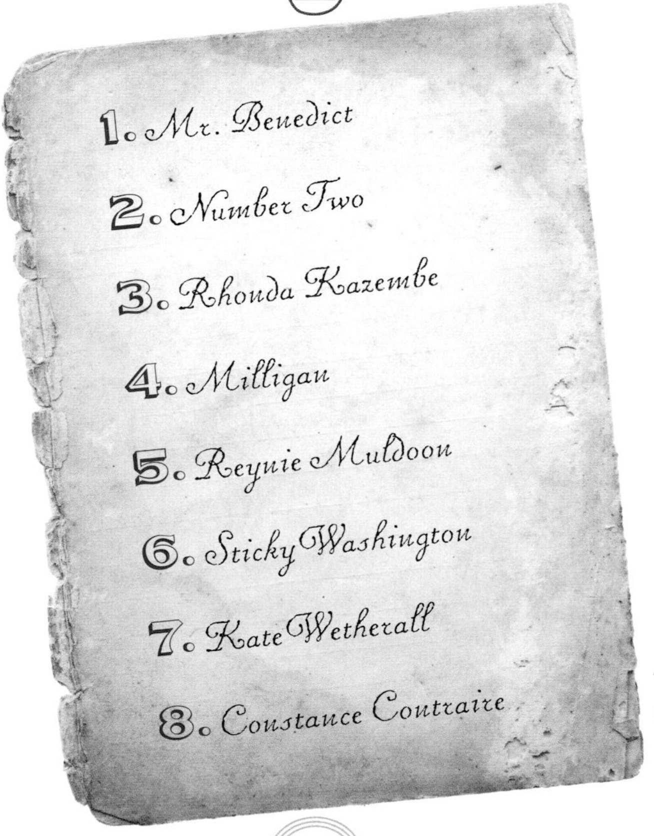

1. Mr. Benedict
2. Number Two
3. Rhonda Kazembe
4. Milligan
5. Reynie Muldoon
6. Sticky Washington
7. Kate Wetherall
8. Constance Contraire

And yet, in these last days, he'd become friends with people who *cared* about him, quite above and beyond what was *expected* of him. With perfect clarity he remembered Reynie saying, "I need you here as a friend." The effect of those words, and of all his friendships, had grown stronger and stronger, until — though he couldn't say *why* he didn't feel mixed up now — at the most desperate moment yet, he knew it to be true. There was bravery in him. It only had to be drawn out.

# THIRD ISLAND PRISON

*With its perfect symmetry — four identical wings, each four stories high, surrounding a bleak courtyard — Third Island Prison is an easy place to get lost.*

One of the Ten Men has hidden an exploding calculator somewhere within the grounds of Third Island Prison. It is set to go off in less than thirty-three minutes.

Will you find it in time?

At your disposal is this coded transmission, which we were fortunate enough to intercept.

Combined with this transmission, you have a map, which, beginning from the top and proceeding row by row, provides a comprehensive view of the grounds.



continued

In what area is the exploding calculator hidden?

___ LETTER ___ NUMBER

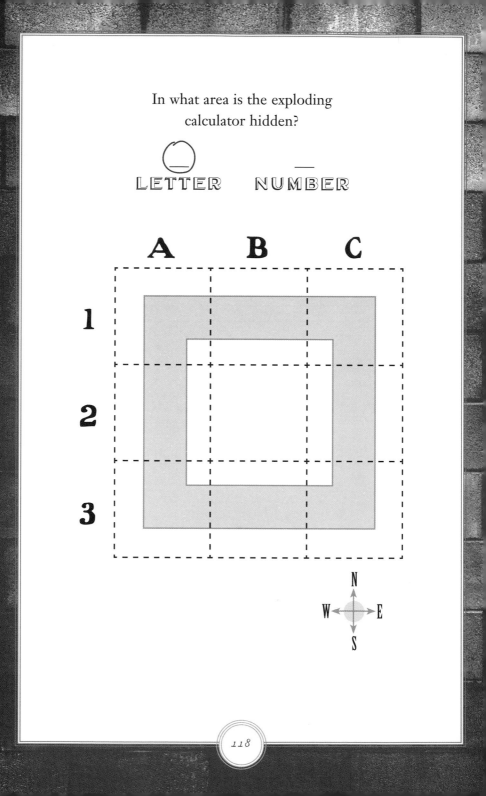

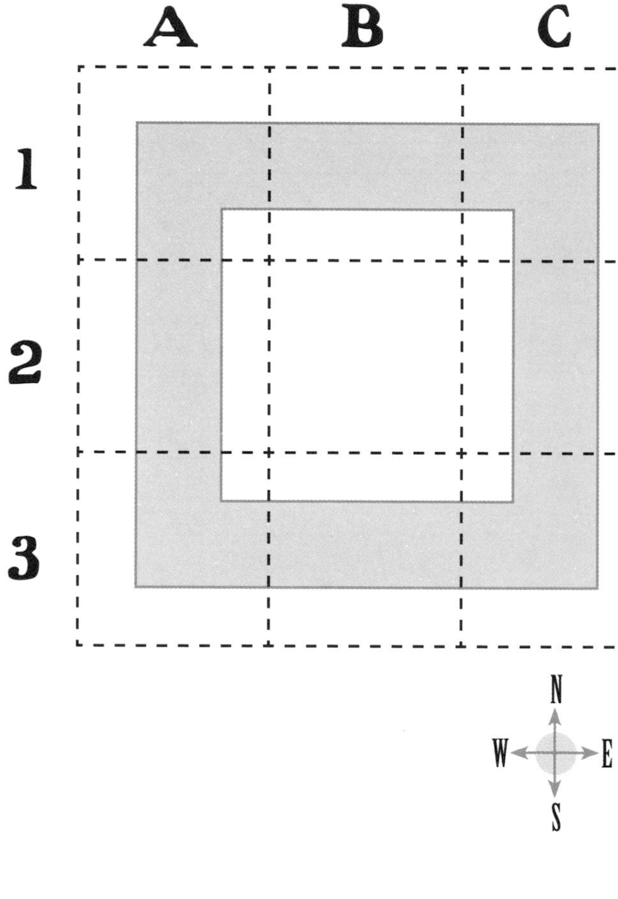

# THE CAPTAIN'S Coordinates

*As Captain Noland will tell you, one's destination is rarely found exactly as expected.*

**Turn the world upside down**
**Though it's north of the equator,**
**And although English is spoken there,**
**Let calculation be your translator.**

COORDINATES

32° 17' 39"

Where is it?

_ _ (_) _ _ _

# GOVERNMENT DOSSIER

TOP SECRET

## MR. CURTAIN'S EXECUTIVES

### WHO ARE THEY?

The designation "Executive" was first used by Mr. Curtain at the Learning Institute for the Very Enlightened, where students observed a strict organizational hierarchy. It referred to former Messengers — students chosen to undergo sessions in Mr. Curtain's Whisperer — who were then entrusted with ongoing managerial duties. It is believed that, over the years, Mr. Curtain dispatched dozens of Executives around the globe to prepare for the Improvement, his plan for total mind control. After the events on Nomansan Island, however, he retained only a small cadre of Executives.

### HOW CAN THEY BE IDENTIFIED?

At L.I.V.E., Executives were identified by their white tunics, blue pants, and blue sashes, but use of such uniforms fell by the wayside after Mr. Curtain fled Nomansan Island. It is believed, however, that some Executives may be easily confused, due to negative effects suffered from repeated sessions in Mr. Curtain's Whisperer. For instance, the dull-minded S.Q. Pedalian is thought to have received the most sessions in the Whisperer; Martina Crowe, the most sharp-minded and aggressive, may have received the fewest.

Jackson and Jillson
S.Q. Pedalian
Martina Crowe

# WINDOWS *and* MIRRORS

*Reynie and I once discussed the notion that where most people see mirrors, others see windows. The key, of course, is to know when there is something behind the glass.*

If this is Mr. Benedict . . .

. . . which one is the mirror?

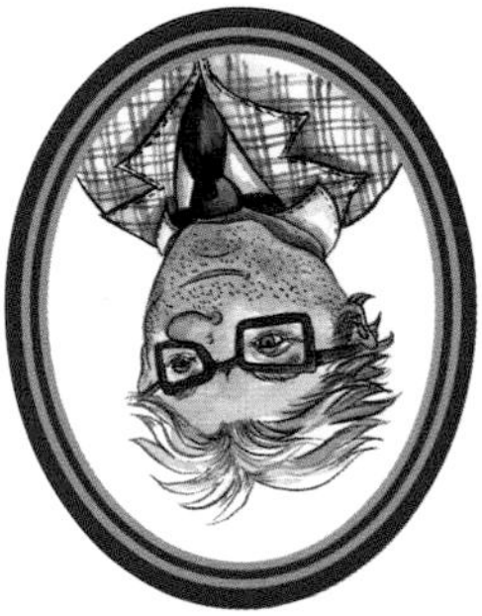

A

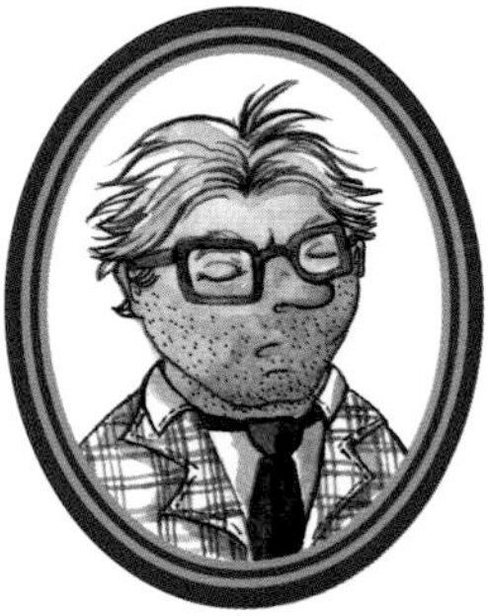

B

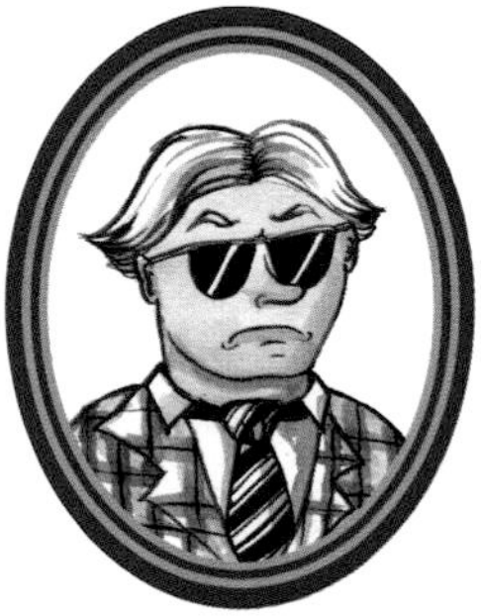

C

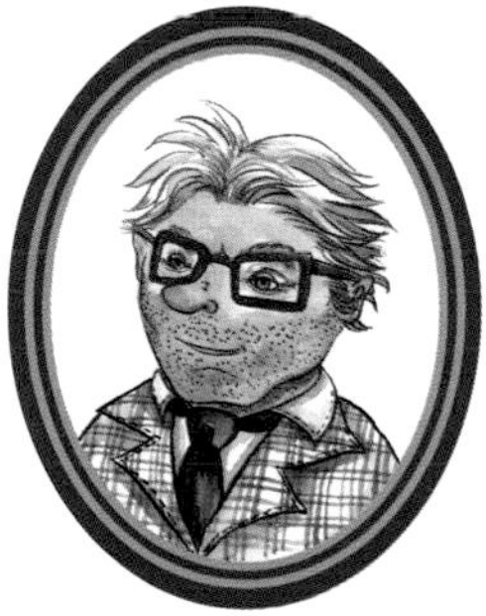

D

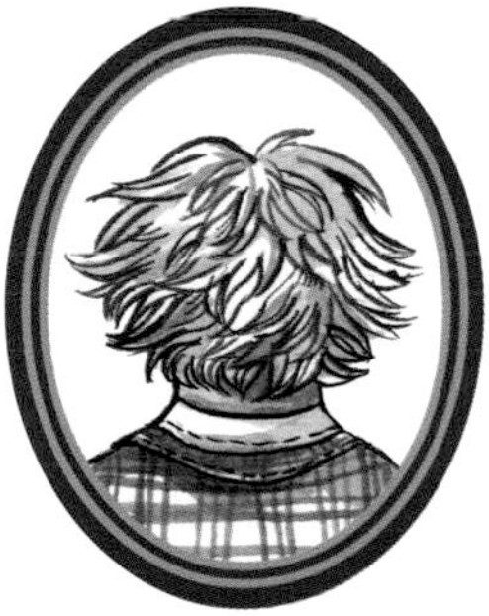

E

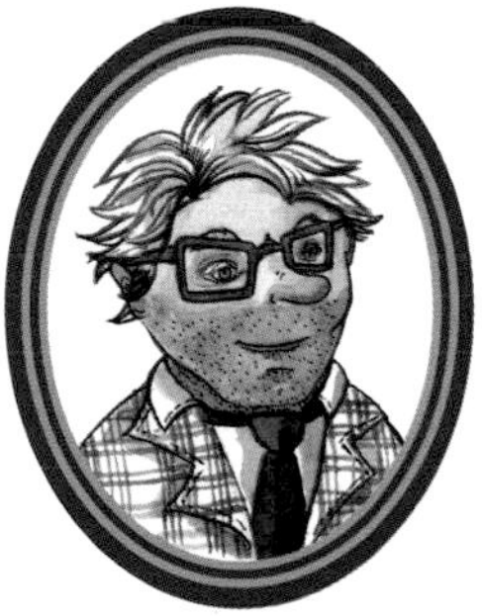

F

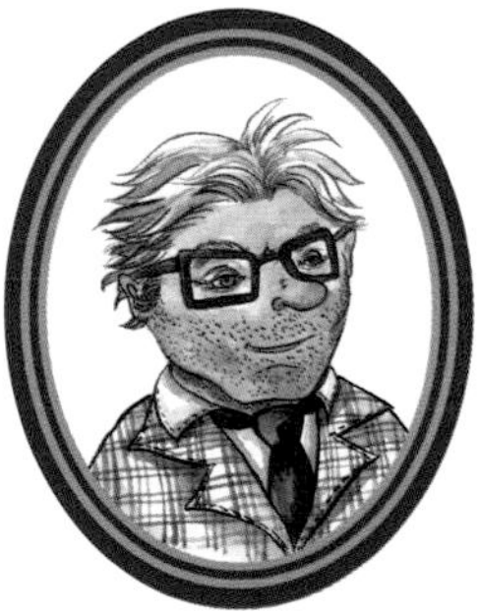

G

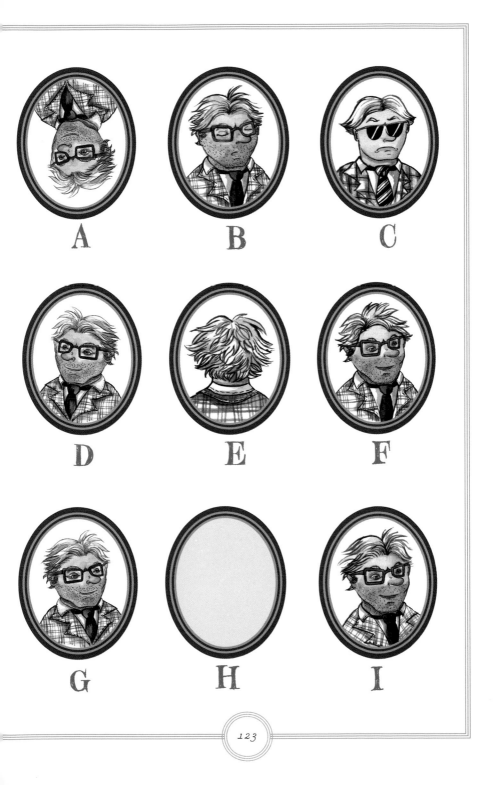

H

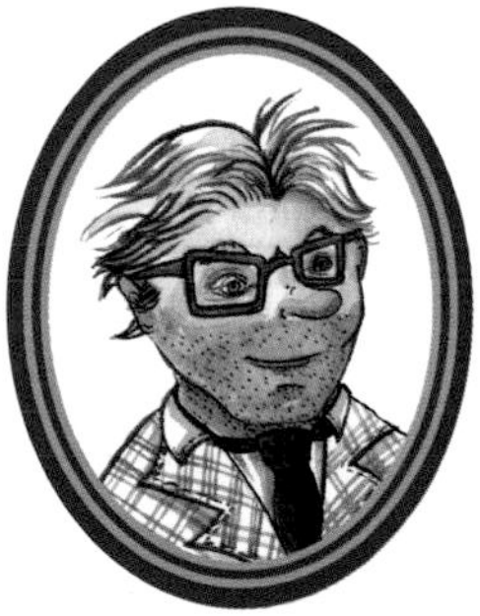

I

# Pencils

*and*

# TRANQUILIZER DARTS

*Children should spend their time learning in absolute safety, particularly when they are learning about danger.*

In a dark room lit only by the beams of two flashlights, Milligan faces a group of Ten Men.

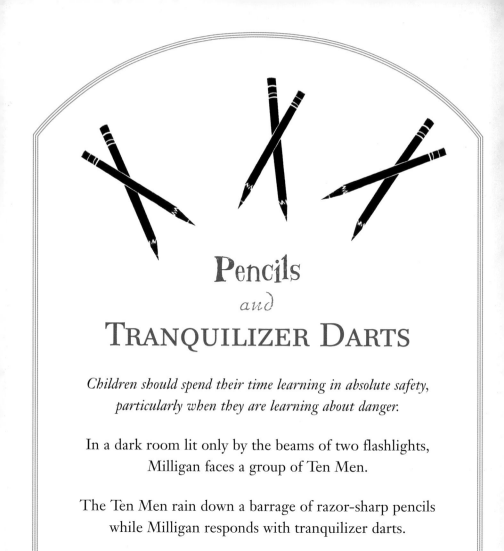

The Ten Men rain down a barrage of razor-sharp pencils while Milligan responds with tranquilizer darts.

Which side of the room is Milligan on?

**L** **R**

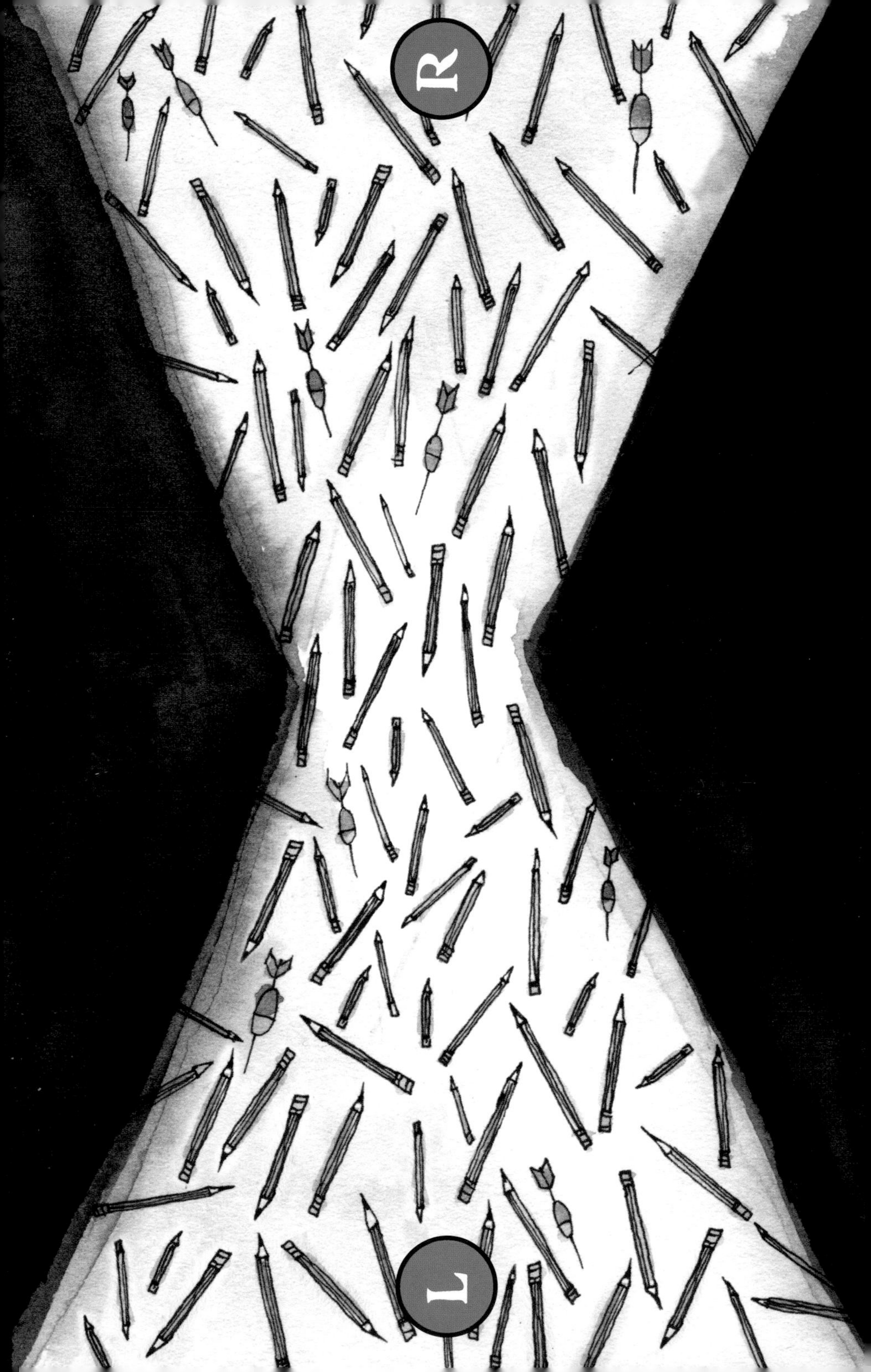
R
L

*On Nomansan Island, Sticky glimpsed a diagram of Mr. Curtain's brain, which served as the model for the Whisperer. Mr. Curtain's notes explaining that diagram, however, were not seen until later, when Kate herself swiped his journal in her final hours at L.I.V.E.*

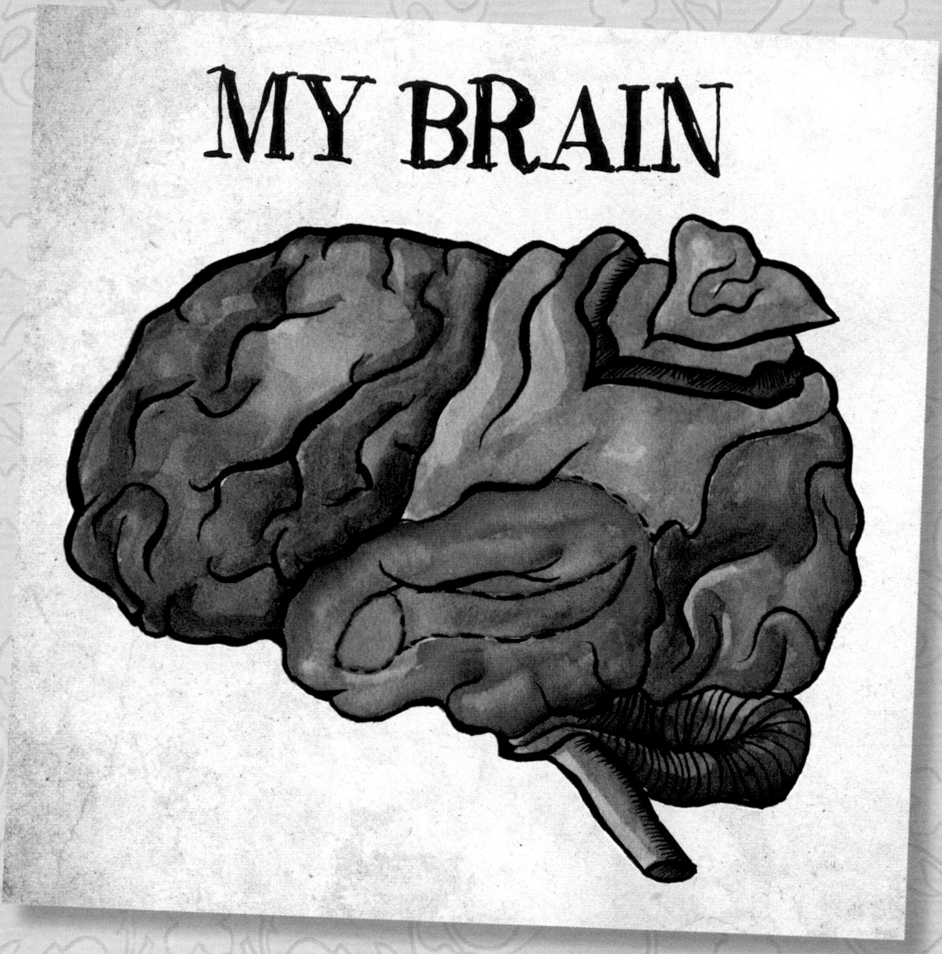

## Frontal lobe

Impressive! This is the top executive behind my every stroke of genius. Naturally underdeveloped in children.

## Amygdala

Highly sensitive to emotions. May be linked to area in cerebral cortex regulating sleep. MUST BE CONTROLLED.

## Hippocampus

My gateway to planting thoughts in the minds of others!

## Temporal lobe

The invaluable vault where my long-term memories are held. Of course, security in most brains is delightfully lax.

## Cerebral cortex

The most intricate and complex area of my brain. I cannot hope to re-create it…only to harness its extraordinary power.

*Over my objections, Rhonda insisted that we include this commendation from my service long ago as a code breaker. No doubt she thought you would be amused to see a picture of me in my younger days. At the time, I was no less proud of orchestrating the inclusion of a small hidden message for a friend. An agreeable clerk in the Commendations office evidently found me as persuasive as our wartime enemy did.*

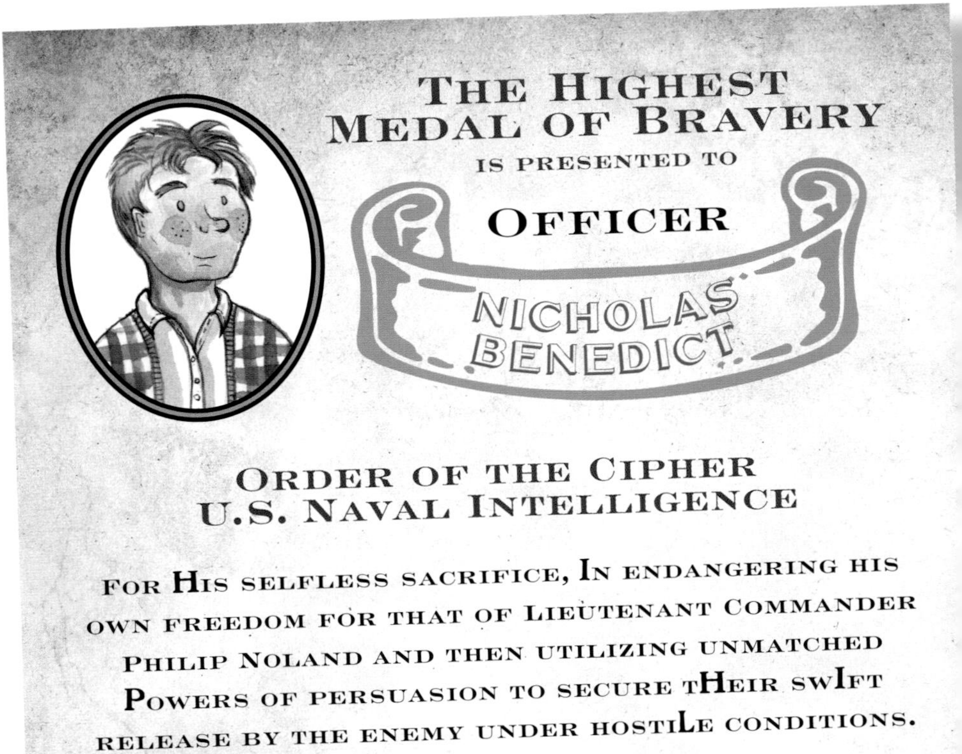

The Highest Medal of Bravery

is presented to

Officer

Nicholas Benedict

Order of the Cipher

U.S. Naval Intelligence

For His selfless sacrifice, In endangering his own freedom for that of Lieutenant Commander Philip Noland and then utilizing unmatched Powers of persuasion to secure tHeir swIft release by the enemy under hostiLe conditions.

Secretary of the U.S. Navy

President of the United States of America

# Nicholas Benedict

**Mentor,**
**The Mysterious Benedict Society**

*Achievements* Last century's Malta Incident; received Stimler Prize for Research in Neuroscience and Philosophy; rarely hit his head when falling asleep; thwarted his brother Mr. Curtain's plans for world domination

*Expertise* Genius

*Habits* Narcolepsy (uncontrollable bouts of sleep) triggered by strong emotion

*History* Born in Holland; after his parents died in a laboratory accident, briefly resided with his aunt in America, then in a series of orphanages; earned multiple university degrees; served as a code breaker in U.S. Naval Intelligence

# THE LAST WORD

*No doubt you will recall my brother's secret password, but he was mistaken about what matters most. Good luck to you! Quickly, now!*

**The key is in each other**
**You know how this must end**
**In Mr. Curtain's nether worlds**
**On this you must depend**

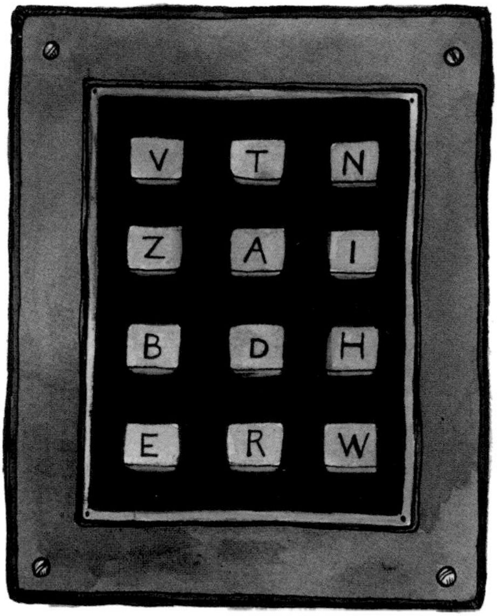


Enter the secret code.

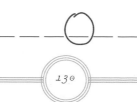

___ ___ ___ (___) ___ ___

# Helpful Resources

# MORSE CODE

| | | | | | |
|---|---|---|---|---|---|
| A | • — | J | • — — — | S | • • • |
| B | — • • • | K | — • — | T | • — — |
| C | • — • | L | • • • — | U | • • — |
| D | — • | M | — — | V | • • • — |
| E | — — • | N | — • • | W | — • — • — |
| F | — • • — | O | — — — | X | — • • — |
| G | • • — • | P | • — — • | Y | — • — — |
| H | — | Q | — — • — | Z | — — • • |
| I | • | R | • — • • | | |

# MORSE CODE

| | | | | | |
|---|---|---|---|---|---|
| A | •– | J | •––– | S | ••• |
| B | –••• | K | –•– | T | – |
| C | –•–• | L | •–•• | U | ••– |
| D | –•• | M | –– | V | •••– |
| E | • | N | –• | W | •–– |
| F | ••–• | O | ––– | X | –••– |
| G | ––• | P | •––• | Y | –•–– |
| H | •••• | Q | ––•– | Z | ––•• |
| I | •• | R | •–• | | |

# COUNTING IN TAMIL

| | | | | | | | | |
|---|---|---|---|---|---|---|---|---|
| 1 | 2 | 3 | 4 | 5 | 6 | 7 | 8 | 9 |
| ௧ | ௨ | ௩ | ௪ | ௫ | ௬ | ௭ | ௮ | ௯ |

Reynie smiled to himself. He was quite familiar with Sticky's habit of polishing his spectacles when nervous, and seeing him do so now was unexpectedly satisfying. There was a unique pleasure in knowing a friend so well, Reynie reflected, rather like sharing a secret code.

# STICKY'S GLOSSARY

**astoundished.** *adj.* a word that does not appear in any of Mr. Benedict's dictionaries, meaning either "astounded" or "astonished"

**baffuddled.** *adj.* a novel coinage meant to describe feeling "baffled" or "befuddled"

**bullfrog.** *n.* a slang term meaning "a proud, puffed-up, self-important individual," typically used by Cannonball to refer to wealthy shipowners

**cacophonous.** *adj.* having a very harsh, discordant, or loud sound

**cataclystrophic.** *adj.* an unsanctioned portmanteau blending "cataclysmic" and "catastrophic"

**cerebrum.** *n.* the largest part of the brain, consisting of both the left and the right hemispheres

**complexicated.** *adj.* a linguistic amalgamation combining "complex" and "complicated"

***controle.*** *n.* a Dutch word meaning "control," which was once used as a secret password by Mr. Curtain

**disperturbed.** *adj.* an accidental mangling of the words "disturbed" and "perturbed"; thought to convey distress

**epidermis.** *n.* the outermost, nonvascular layer of skin; in plants, refers to the outer integument

**follicular.** *adj.* relating to a tiny cavity, usually one that sprouts hair

**fungal.** *adj.* relating to mushrooms, molds, mildews, rusts, or smuts

**gossamer.** *adj.* extremely light, gauzy, fine, filmy, or thin

**gutter.** *n.* a term used in book publishing to indicate the inside margins between two pages that face each other



continued

**hyphae.** *n.* elements emanating from the spores of fungi

**infuritating.** *adj.* an awkward neologism meant to describe something that is either "infuriating" or "irritating"

**innoventive.** *adj.* an unintentional comingling of "inventive" and "innovative"

**inspectigate.** *adj.* a mistaken construction that jumbles two similar words, "inspect" and "investigate"

**multitude.** *n.* a very large number of people; a profusion

**panache.** *n.* a very stylish, flamboyant, enthusiastic, or dynamic manner; élan

**repellsive.** *adj.* an unwitting verbal entanglement of the adjectives "repellent" and "repulsive"

**sovereignty.** *n.* royal status or authority; a supreme independent power

**transfer protocol.** *n.* also known as hypertext transfer protocol, a universal standard for addressing websites on the Internet, including www.mysteriousbenedictsociety.com

**undomesticated.** *adj.* untamed or wild; unaccustomed to living in accordance with cultural norms

**unsuitisfactory.** *adj.* an invented word thought to derive from confusion between "unsuitable" and "unsatisfactory"

**urchin.** *n.* a mischievous young person; distinct from a "sea urchin," which is any echinoderm of the class Echinoidea

***vriend.*** *n.* a Dutch word meaning "friend"

# HINTS

**PAGE 4**
What letters are missing from the classified advertisements?

**PAGE 5**
Solve the code twice, using each of the Morse codes in the Helpful Resources section. Which side is the right one on?

**PAGE 6**
Follow the middle of the three digits printed on the page, in the direction of the arrow. Repeat.

**PAGE 22**
Weather all. Con tray air. Wash in ton. Mull dune.

**PAGE 24**
See *The Exhaustive Encyclopedia of Sleep*.

**PAGE 28**
Turn one on its head, and fold another.

**PAGE 30**
If you keep dividing a number in half, will you ever reach zero?

**PAGE 32**
Look to the letters directly above the contrary answers.

**PAGE 34**
Don't read the lines in order. Follow their instructions instead.

**PAGE 35**
Tic-tac-toe.

**PAGE 36**
Which floor feels like an icebox?

**PAGE 43**
The slingshot hit the wasps' nest. The marbles tripped up everyone. The whistle called for Madge, who took the man's toupee. The rope was thrown to them, but it was covered in glue. The bucket dumped the water.



continued

**PAGE 50**
If you start with the square button, only one is left unaccounted for.

**PAGE 56**
One of these a day won't keep the dentist away.

**PAGE 58** - - - - - - - - - - >

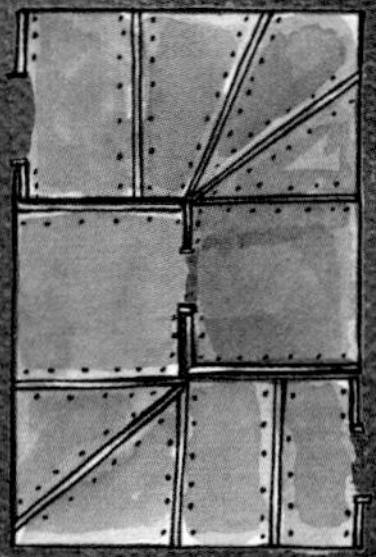

**PAGE 60**
Look behind you. What does every normal room have?

**PAGE 62**
All snacks and meals were eaten in reverse alphabetical order — except one.

**PAGE 67**
Follow the sentries' pointing fingers.

**PAGE 72**
"Glossary" is not a mangling of "gloss" and "dictionary," but that does not mean you won't find it helpful in this instance.

## PAGE 78

Draw a ninety-degree angle that emanates from the wall. One of its rays must meet the end of the transmitter, while the other ray meets the Whisperer.

## PAGE 80

While Moocho holds the pies, Kate has her bucket.

## PAGE 82

Look in Constance's notebook.

## PAGE 85

Using the chart in the Helpful Resources, write the numbers corresponding to the symbols in each box of a Tamil square. Which number is missing?

## PAGE 89

"And Jill came tumbling after."

## PAGE 90

Mr. Pressius would not want you to fold each corner into the middle to see what was stolen.



continued

**PAGE 92**
Look up the page number of this challenge in the book's Table of Contents.

**PAGE 93**
No one said the kindhearted genius was a man.

**PAGE 95**
The key lies in the second word, which appears backward. Hold it up to itself to see.

**PAGE 101**
Mr. Curtain's Whisperer has no leg cuffs.

**PAGE 104**
Stack *T* in another bucket. But which one?

**PAGE 106**
Read the first letter of each line.

**PAGE 109**
Count by sevens.

## PAGE 112
Fold the pages together.

## PAGE 115
Her name is Pencilla.

## PAGE 117
Place the letters into the squares of the map, row by row.

## PAGE 119
Read the coordinates upside down on a calculator, like the one hidden on the grounds of Third Island Prison.

## PAGE 122
Reverse the picture.

## PAGE 124
From which side are the darts originating?

## PAGE 130
The end of this word is *end*, even in Dutch, which is spoken in the Netherlands.

"Have you not proven yourselves once again to be the bravest, most resourceful children in the world?"

## "Remember, children. For every exit, there is also an entrance."

*Upon completion of the preceding exercises, you are ready to make yours.*

__ __ __    __ __ __    __ __ __ __ __
*32 32 32    90 113 93    4 4 102 122 73*

__    __ __    __ __ __ __ __ __ __ __ .
*115    80 50    18 26 58 58 58 58 30 57*

__ __ __ __ __ __    __ __ __
*35 110 92 119 60 23    89 95 83*

__ __ __ __ __ __ __ __
*104 47 25 62 139 139 29 78*

__ __ __ __ __ __ __ __    __ __
*76 76 76 107 107 118 67 34    65 65*

__ __ __    __ __ __ __ .
*40 40 40    98 5 85 130*

After a few more pages of questions, all of which Reynie felt confident he had answered correctly, he arrived at the test's final question: "Are you brave?" Just reading the words quickened Reynie's heart. Was he brave? Bravery had never been required of him, so how could he tell? Miss Perumal would say he was: She would point out how cheerful he tried to be despite feeling lonely, how patiently he withstood the teasing of other children, and how he was always eager for a challenge. But these things only showed that he was good-natured, polite, and very often bored. Did they really show that he was brave? He didn't think so. Finally he gave up trying to decide and simply wrote, "I hope so."

*Upon reflection, you will see what is coming.*

Turn the page for a sneak peek at

# The Extraordinary Education of Nicholas Benedict

Coming in 2012

# A Beginning at the End

The train station at Pebbleton, dark and sooty though it was, glistened in the mist. Electric lamps above the platform cast their light upon a thousand reflecting surfaces: the puddles along the tracks, the streaked windows of the station house, the umbrellas hoisted over huddled, indistinct figures on the platform. To a person of whimsical mind, the scene might resemble something from a tale, a magical gathering in a dark wood, the umbrellas looming like toadstools over fairy folk.

There was, in fact, such a person watching from the window of the approaching train, a boy of whimsical mind, to be sure (though whimsy was not the half of it, nor even the beginning), and the fairy-tale qualities of the scene occurred to him at once. So too did a great many other things, including the sentence "*It glistened in the mist; the train hissed, and I listened*," a poetic train of thought that sounded rather like a train itself, which pleased him. But foremost in the boy's mind was the awareness that Pebbleton station was his stop — the end of his train journey, the beginning of a new unknown.

He turned to his chaperone, a plump old woman with spectacles so large the brim of her hat rested upon their frames. "What shall we call this, Mrs. Ferrier — an arrival or a departure?"

Mrs. Ferrier was putting away her knitting needles. "I suppose both, Nicholas. Or however you like." She clasped her bag and peered out the grimy window. "It's a miserable night for either."

"Shall I tell you what I'm thinking, Mrs. Ferrier?"

"Heavens no, Nicholas! That would take hours, and we have only moments. There, we've stopped."

The old woman turned from the window to appraise his appearance, despite having already done so before they boarded the train. Nicholas doubted he had changed much in the course of their half day's journey, and his reflection, easily seen in Mrs. Ferrier's enormous spectacles, proved him right: He was still a skinny, towheaded nine-year-old with threadbare clothes and an unfortunate nose. Indeed, his nose was so long and lumpy that it drew attention away from his one good feature — his bright and impish green eyes — though Mrs. Ferrier had often remarked that someday, should Nicholas come to require spectacles, his nose would do an admirable job holding them in place. It was always best to be positive, she told him.

"Well?" he asked as she studied him. "Do you think they'll take me? Or will they send me back and keep the money for their trouble?"

Mrs. Ferrier pursed her lips. "Please don't be saucy, Nicholas. I say this for your sake. It's nothing to *me* now, is it? Remember your manners, and make yourself useful around the orphanage. Start off on the right foot, and you'll be happier for it."

Nicholas feigned surprise. "Oh! You want me to be happy, Mrs. Ferrier?"

"Of course I do," puffed the old woman as she struggled to her feet. "I want everyone to be happy, don't I? Now follow me, and mind you don't step on the backs of my shoes."

Mrs. Ferrier and Nicholas were the only passengers to disembark the train. Several were boarding, however, and they crowded the aisles most inconveniently as they closed their umbrellas and removed their overcoats. By the time the old woman and her charge managed to descend the steps, the platform was empty save for one man in a somber gray suit and hat, standing rigidly beneath his umbrella. At the sight of them, he strode forward to shield Mrs. Ferrier with it. He was so tall that when he stood over Nicholas his face appeared mostly as a sharp, jutting chin and cavernous nostrils. His suit carried a faintly pleasant odor of pipe tobacco, which Nicholas liked, and the boy's initial impression was neutral until Mr. Collum, which was the man's name, introduced himself to Mrs. Ferrier and told Nicholas to run and fetch his trunk.

"There's no trunk to fetch, sir," said Nicholas, blinking in the mist (for he stood outside the umbrella's protection). "Only this suitcase. I'm Nicholas, sir. Nicholas Benedict." He held out his hand.

"No trunk?" said Mr. Collum, frowning. "Well, I daresay that's common enough, though I hadn't expected it. I haven't met a child at the station before, you see." He was speaking directly to Mrs. Ferrier and appeared not to have noticed Nicholas's outstretched hand. "I assumed directorship of the Manor only this spring, as I'm sure Mr. Cuckieu told you."

"The Manor?" said Mrs. Ferrier with a confused look.

"Forgive me," Mr. Collum said. "You must know the

orphanage as Rothschild's End — or 'Child's End, as it is often abbreviated. In these parts, however, it is quite common to shorten the name still further, for ease of speaking, and to refer to the place simply as the Manor. The residence at 'Child's End is the only manor in the area, you see, so this leads to no confusion."

Nicholas began to ask a question, but though he spoke clearly and politely enough, Mr. Collum continued speaking to Mrs. Ferrier as if Nicholas hadn't uttered a word.

"Now, madam," Mr. Collum said, "allow me to accompany you inside the station house, where you can wait out of the damp. I would invite you to the Manor for refreshment, but I'm afraid it's quite a long ride from Pebbleton. Our kettle would hardly have begun to whistle before your train does — it's due to arrive at nine."

Nicholas and Mrs. Ferrier, who was trying not to look shattered at the prospect of waiting in the station house for two hours, followed Mr. Collum into a dim, drafty room with sawdust on the floor and benches along the walls. Near the ticket counter, the stationmaster was telling the train conductor about a wicked egg thief who had visited his barn the night before. The conductor, seeing that Mrs. Ferrier and Nicholas had disembarked at last, gestured at the clock, and the stationmaster accompanied him back out to the train, hurrying to finish his story. The newcomers were left alone with a red-haired man who sat on one of the benches, absorbed in a rain-spotted newspaper.

"May I just have a brief word with you, Mr. Collum?" asked Mrs. Ferrier. "A private word?"

"Of course," said Mr. Collum, who had yet to look directly at Nicholas but did seem aware of him, for he held up a finger to indicate that the boy should stay put. He drew Mrs. Ferrier over to the ticket counter, where they stood with their backs to the room and spoke in hushed voices.

Nicholas strained his ears but could not make out a word, so he turned his attention to the red-haired newspaper reader. The man appeared to be of late middle age, perhaps a decade older than Mr. Collum. His tanned, rough hands suggested a different sort of labor from that which occupied the orphanage director (whose own pale fingers were carefully manicured and, excepting one inky smear, as clean as soap could make them). A faint impression in the man's hair suggested he'd been wearing a hat, though Nicholas saw none on the bench, nor any on the hat rack nearby. With some difficulty the man turned to a different section in his newspaper (the damp pages clung together) and resumed his reading, mouthing the words to himself. Nicholas, watching his lips, followed along for a tedious ten seconds ("... *impact on the price of wheat since the war's conclusion* ...") before losing patience and interest.

He glanced at the schedule above the ticket counter. Mrs. Ferrier's nine o'clock train was just the fifth one of the day; it was also the last. Pebbleton, it seemed, was not quite on the way to anywhere. Nicholas stepped to the nearest window facing the street. At the curb sat an aged Studebaker with mud on its tires and steam rising from its hood. Beyond it Nicholas could see most of Pebbleton without moving his head. A handful of shops, a few market stalls closed down for the day, an occasional parked automobile. In the gloomy distance, a grain silo put Nicholas in mind of a lighthouse seen through fog. A glary smudge over the trees to the west was all the sunset the evening could muster.

Behind the station house, the train sounded its whistle. Nicholas perked up his ears, hoping the adults would raise their voices. Naturally he was curious to know what they were saying about him. But the clamor of the departing train was so overwhelming that Nicholas couldn't have heard them if they shouted. The windows rattled; the plank floors trembled. Then a ghostly reflection appeared in the window behind his own, and Nicholas turned to discover Mrs. Ferrier looking down on him with grave finality. Mr. Collum lingered at the ticket counter, checking his pocket watch against the station house clock.

For what would be the last time, the old woman and young boy regarded each other. They were compelled to wait for the train to finish leaving the station before attempting to speak, however, which gave Nicholas ample time to reflect upon the occasion. He had wondered what sort of expression Mrs. Ferrier would put on for their parting, and now that the moment was at hand, he found it to be rather what he had expected: polite, businesslike, and almost comically serious. She was serious for his sake, he knew, in case he was afraid or sad. She was not much attached to Nicholas, perhaps because of his habitual impertinence — she thought him too saucy by far — but Mrs. Ferrier believed there was a way of doing things, and because she took comfort in this belief, she always made an effort.

She need not have bothered, at least not for Nicholas's sake. He was anything but sad. The last orphanage had been the worst yet, and he was glad to leave it. In fact, his time there had been so awful that before his departure he had secretly deposited sardines in many a tormentor's pillowcase, and had clicked his heels as he went out the door. No, he was far from sad, and though certainly nervous, he was not afraid, either. Or not *very* afraid, anyway. The Manor could hardly be worse than the last place, and there was always the chance it would be better.

The train's caboose had not yet cleared the station when the redheaded man rose, stretched, rearranged his newspaper, and exited the station house. Mr. Collum, meanwhile, had finished adjusting his watch and tucked it away. He went to the open door and paused. Glancing at Mrs. Ferrier, he touched his hat in what appeared to be a courteous farewell — though he might simply have been lowering its brim against the weather — and stepped outside with his umbrella. All of this had occurred as if in pantomime, with the train's rumbling, screeching, and clattering crowding out all other sound. When at last something like silence returned to the station house, Mrs. Ferrier laid a hand on the boy's shoulder.

"Nicholas, you know what you must do," she said.

"Oh yes, Mrs. Ferrier! I'm to carry my suitcase out to that Studebaker, and never mind the drizzle. I imagine I'll sit in the back while Mr. Collum rides in front with the driver."

Mrs. Ferrier blinked. "The driver?"

"Why, sure," said Nicholas with a shrug. "That red-haired man with the new hat."

"The red-haired man . . ." Straightening, Mrs. Ferrier looked out the window behind him. Her eyebrows rose in surprise. "Well, yes, you're correct, though it isn't at all what I was going to say. I was going to say . . ." She noticed the boy staring at her expectantly, the corners of his lips twitching as if he was suppressing a smile, and she sighed. "Oh, very well, Nicholas. Tell me how you knew all that. This will be my last opportunity to hear one of your exhausting explanations."

Nicholas grinned, raised his chin like a songbird preparing to sing, and throwing his arms out for emphasis, burst forth with an astonishing flurry of words: "Well, the hat *must* be new, don't you think? Otherwise he wouldn't have left it in the Studebaker to spare it getting wet. Which is a funny thing, in my opinion, since hats are meant to protect their owners and not the other way around. But I've known quite a lot of people who go to amazing trouble on behalf of their hats, haven't you, Mrs. Ferrier? I wonder what happened to his umbrella, though? Perhaps he lost it. Anyway, I do wish he'd left a section of the newspaper for me — to cover my head with, you know, as he did, to keep it dry."

"I'm sure he meant to," said the old woman after a confused pause, "but only forgot." (This was the sort of thing Mrs. Ferrier always said in such cases, as part of her effort to be positive.) "But how did you know he was Mr. Collum's driver?"

Nicholas laughed. It was a squeaky, stuttering laugh, rather like the nickering of a pony. "I certainly doubt he's a passenger! The next train doesn't arrive for two hours, so it's not likely he was waiting for that, is it? Besides, he left when Mr. Collum did, and where else would he be going in this weather if not to that old Studebaker at the curb? It obviously just got here from somewhere out in the country — its engine is still hot and there's mud on the tires — and Mr. Collum said it's a long ride to the Manor. He did say *ride* rather than *drive*, you know, so I got the feeling he didn't intend to sit behind the wheel himself. Now, if there had been horses outside, especially a horse with an umbrella stand attached to it" — here Nicholas nickered again — "I might have come to a different . . ."

Mrs. Ferrier was shaking her head, a common enough response to everything Nicholas said that he would have continued his speech unabated had she not held up a hand to check him. He'd been about to explain half a dozen other reasons he'd come to this conclusion about the red-haired man, as well as several he hadn't consciously thought of yet but which were sure to occur to him as he spoke. But Nicholas was used to being shushed by Mrs. Ferrier, and at any rate he knew that delaying Mr. Collum would not serve him well. So he let the explanations go with a shrug, and waited for Mrs. Ferrier to proceed.

"Thank you, Nicholas. That will be more than enough

to make my poor head ache for the next two hours." Mrs. Ferrier cleared her throat. "And now this is goodbye. When I said that you know what you must do, I only meant to remind you to hold your tongue in check, and to make yourself useful. There, that's the last I'll say." She lifted his chin with her finger and looked once more into his eyes — a little wonderingly at first, as if she saw some mystery there she could never hope to fathom, and then with a different sort of expression Nicholas hadn't seen in her eyes before, something between sadness and exhaustion. She said, "I wish you better luck, child. Better luck than you've had. Now go on. Don't keep Mr. Collum waiting."

"*Au revoir* and *adios*, Mrs. Ferrier!" said Nicholas spryly, offering her an exaggerated military salute.

Mrs. Ferrier flinched and rubbed her temples, for Nicholas truly had given her a headache. Not for the first time she wondered how the boy could seem to know so much and yet so little. Here, at their final parting, he couldn't think of more suitable things to say? No best wishes, not even a word of thanks? No, he only spun on his heels, grabbed his suitcase, and marched out into the next chapter of his life, a brash young soldier headed into a battle he felt certain of winning. He never even looked back.

Unlike her former young charge — now kicking the door closed behind him with a shocking bang — poor Mrs. Ferrier could *not* have thought of more suitable words for the occasion. Nicholas Benedict did have an exceptional gift for knowing things (more exceptional, in fact, than most adults would have thought possible), and yet not even he could know that this next chapter was to be the most unusual — and most important — of his entire childhood. Indeed, the strange days that lay ahead would change him forever, though for now they had less substance than the mist through which he ran.

Misery and joy. Discovery and danger. Mystery and treasure. For now, all were secrets waiting to be revealed.

For now, Nicholas Benedict was just a remarkable young orphan with secrets of his own, hastening to the Studebaker, where Mr. Collum sat in the front passenger seat looking impatient, and the red-haired driver was adjusting the rearview mirror, the better to admire his new hat.